BOOK THREE

MINDSPACE

OFFENSIVE

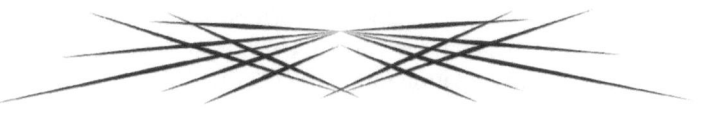

A K DUBOFF

OFFENSIVE
Text Copyright © 2018 by A.K. DuBoff

www.cadicle.com

Published by Dawnrunner Press
Cover Copyright © 2021 A.K. DuBoff

ISBN-10: 1954344139
ISBN-13: 978-1954344136
Copyright Registration Number: TX0008730706

0 9 8 7 6 5 4 3

Produced in the United States of America

TABLE OF CONTENTS

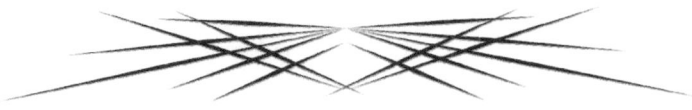

KEY TERMS, CAST & LOCATIONS

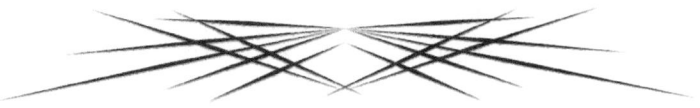

KEY TERMS

Taran – The race of all people in the Taran Empire; synonymous with human

Tararian Guard – The primary military force for the Taran Empire

Jump – Faster-than-light travel through subspace

Beacon Network – The navigation method for subspace jumps, maintained by SiNavTech

High Dynasties – The seven ruling families of the Taran Empire, collectively a governing council

Tararian Selective Service (TSS) – A quasi-military organization specializing in telekinesis; a complement to the Tararian Guard

Telepathic Receptor (TR) – An artificial neural structure that makes an individual susceptible to remote telepathic control

Priesthood – The former governing body of the Taran Empire

CAST

Tararian Guard

Kira Elsar – Captain, team leader

Ari Lanmore – Lance corporal, weapons specialist on Kira's team

Kyle Asher – Lance corporal, technical specialist on Kira's team

Nia Boro – Lance corporal, technical specialist on Kira's team

Lucas Sandren – Major, Kira's commanding officer

Terence Kaen – Colonel, Kira's chain-of-command (formerly possessed by an alien presence known as 'Nox')

Leon Caletti – Civilian consultant, geneticist/scientist, Kira's significant other

Jack – Technical specialist in Leon's lab

Tess – Technical specialist in Leon's lab

Deanna Olvera – Major, Orion Station head of security

Doctor Elric – Lead medical doctor for Orion Station base

Allen Lucian – General, leader of Orion Station base

Crew of the *Raven*

Rodrick – Captain
Aleya – First Officer
Sven – Support systems engineer
Gil – Mechanic

Elusian Alliance *(member world of Taran Empire)*

Elton Joris – President

Ellen Caletti – Press Secretary, former Mysaran spy (Leon's sister)
Nico – Assistant to President Joris

Mysaran Coalition *(independent world)*

Cynthia Hale – Former Mysaran chancellor (deceased, formerly possessed by an alien presence known as 'Reya')

MTech *(Research company based on Mysar; branch on Valta)*

Monica Waylon – Director of MTech's lab on Valta (deceased)

Jared Frey – Monica's research assistant at the MTech lab

(formerly possessed by an alien presence known as 'Nox')

LOCATIONS

Orion Station – Tararian Guard base

Elvar Trinary – Kira's home system (planets: Mysar, Valta, Elusia)

Gaelon System — Supposedly uninhabited star system adjacent to the Elvar Trinary

Tararia – The central planet of the Taran Empire

CHAPTER 1

KIRA SAW THE punch coming as if it was in slow motion. She dove aside, easily avoiding the swing. "You'll have to try harder than that," she needled her sparring partner.

Ari, the weapons specialist on her covert ops team, grunted. "I'm going easy on you."

Kira smirked. "Sure you are."

In the week since Kira had been exposed to the experimental nanites developed by MTech, she'd experienced a new level of physical ability unlike anything she'd dreamed was possible. Strength, endurance, speed, reflexes—her years of physical training and conditioning hadn't come close to granting such mastery. But, thanks to her new nanotech upgrades, now she could even rival someone of Ari's substantial stature in combat.

The odds are evened.

With a determined glint in her eyes, she got a running start to slide across the floor toward Ari. Her legs deftly wrapped around his, and she snatched ahold of his right wrist while he toppled to the side.

She pinned him. "I bet you let me do that, too, huh?"

Ari struggled against her with no effect. "I'm not sure I like this new you."

Kira released him. *I'm not sure I do, either.*

She had come to terms early in her Guard career that mental prowess was the greatest asset she could contribute to a team. She had been able to keep up in training and combat, but being a living tank was never a consideration. Now, her sense of identity was at a crossroads. Her new physical abilities had a catch—a big one.

Whenever she became too agitated and lost focus, she would transform into a Robus. The hybrid alien form shouldn't even be possible, and yet it was her new reality. While she had remained lucid during her latest transformation, the technology was unstable; she had no control over the timing of the form shift. In addition, the agony she had experienced during past transformations didn't exactly encourage her to make it a regular occurrence.

Moreover, it was the enemy who wanted her to master the form. The Guard soldier in her screamed that she should run away from the enemy's designs for her fate, but she couldn't avoid what was inside her.

"Hey, I was only joking," Ari said when Kira didn't reply.

"Yeah, I know." She took a slow breath. "This is weird for me, too."

Ari stretched out his shoulder. "You'll get used to it eventually."

"Unless I decide not to."

He eyed her. "You mean that suppression therapy Leon invented?"

"You heard about that?" Kira raised an eyebrow.

"Word gets around. I mean, our team *does* specialize in

information gathering."

"Fair point." She shook her head. "Yeah, he came up with something, but I'm not crazy about trying more experimental shite."

"Don't blame you. Plus, there's that whole part about you now being able to take me down." Ari grinned.

"Not a bad side effect, not gonna lie."

Ari shrugged. "You haven't randomly transformed since Mysar, so maybe—"

"It's not that I don't think I could gain control of the shifting," Kira interrupted. "I'm even willing to deal with the pain of the transformation. But there are some other really big things that we keep overlooking because aspects of this seem good on the surface."

"Such as?" Ari prompted.

"Well, the obvious thing: that psycho-bitch doctor, Monica, intentionally did this to me. Those aliens in Gaelon want me for something, and I don't particularly want to find out what they're planning."

"Admittedly, that part isn't ideal."

"You think?" Kira groaned. "But let's pretend for a minute that we can thwart their plan and I don't somehow become a weapon for their dastardly ends. Best-case scenario, I have enhanced strength and speed, and I can transform into the Robus form at will. But, whenever I try to transform, my track record is either having a seizure or entering into a temporary blind rage. Either way, in a battle scenario, that means I'd be a massive liability to the team."

"Regardless of that, Kira, the bigger question here is what you're comfortable doing. You need to decide if you want to embrace your changes or have them go away. This half-committed thing is probably what's causing most of your issues."

"The threat those aliens in Gaelon pose isn't in my head."

Ari chuckled. "Well, they certainly would like to be."

She sighed. "Okay, that was poor phrasing for a comment about telepathic beings. But you know what I mean."

He nodded. "They want you for something, and we don't know what that is."

"Exactly."

"So, when are we going to go find out?"

Kira laughed. "Aren't you jumping ahead a little?"

Ari evaluated her. "Rumor has it that you traced the telepathic signal in Jared before you evicted the Nox entity."

Only a handful of people were privy to that information. "How did you…?"

"You might want to talk to Leon about keeping his mouth shut." Ari gave Kira a playful smile.

And this is why we don't typically have civilians work with the Guard. Kira nodded. "What if we *did* trace that signal back?"

"That's obvious. You're going after them."

She'd already said too much to outright deny what she knew. "Maybe. The signal trace confirmed that Gaelon is where the beings are camped out, but I haven't heard anything from the Guard leadership yet about next steps."

"Maybe they needed to run it higher up the chain."

Kira shrugged. "Or maybe they decided that it's a remote enough system that it's not worth the trouble to investigate."

"Did one of my punches actually connect with your head today?" Ari asked. "Since when does the Guard know about a threat and not do something about it?"

"Maybe it's just wishful thinking."

"I thought you *wanted* this?"

"I do." Kira crossed her arms. "It's complicated."

Ari leaned against the wall and tilted his head.

"I want to go after the bad guys that did this to me, don't get me wrong," she explained. "But I can't shake this feeling that this was all part of some master plan, and we'd be walking into a trap."

"You've overpowered both of the beings we've encountered, and you can do it again," Ari tried to assure her.

"That was when they were remotely projecting themselves," Kira countered. "Going to Gaelon, we'd be on their turf. And that is *precisely* where Kaen tried to take me while he was subverted."

"It's risky, yes, but we can't ignore a threat in a system that neighbors a Taran Empire world."

"I know."

"And that's why you'll have us with you." Ari smiled.

"I really don't like the idea of you walking into a trap with me."

"It's not a trap if we can avoid it together."

Kira nodded.

The training room door opened, and Nia poked her head inside. "Colonel wants to meet with us."

Kira came to attention. "About what?"

"Sandren didn't say when he relayed the order, but I got the impression it's for recon."

"Sounds like they've made the decision for us," Ari said to Kira.

"It does." She grabbed her water bottle from the rack and took a swig.

"You know what this is about?" Nia asked her.

"I'll give you one guess."

The soldier nodded. "Right. I should have known."

Kira looked down at her mussed shipsuit from the

sparring. "I don't suppose we have time to clean up?"

"Meeting is ASAP," Nia replied.

"Classic."

Kira smoothed her suit and re-styled her short, red hair as best she could while they walked down the hall to the designated briefing room. It wouldn't be the first time she showed up to a meeting directly following a workout, and it likely wouldn't be the last.

When they arrived, Kyle, Major Sandren, and Colonel Kaen were waiting for them around the table.

"Sirs," Kira greeted the two officers.

"Thank you for the prompt arrival, Captain," Kaen replied.

"Of course, sir." Kira took the chair closest to the door.

"I'm sure you've already guessed why we're meeting," Sandren stated as soon as everyone was settled. "We need to address Gaelon."

Kaen nodded. "We've rolled out testing for the telepathic receptor—or TR—neural structures Leon and his team identified, but Guard leadership has deemed future telepathic assaults to be too big a risk for us to move past this incident without further investigation. We're authorizing a recon mission to Gaelon so you can see what we're up against."

Kira's chest tightened. "Yes, sir."

"I'll accompany you on the *Raven*," Sandren continued. "Our long-range scan indicates that there's at least one, or possibly two, planetary bodies in the system. There's some strange radiation that's made it difficult to get an accurate assessment."

"So, we run an in-system scan and report back?" Kira asked.

"This might require an on-the-ground investigation," Kaen replied. "You mentioned that the alien, Reya, shared a vision of a planet with you. If you do find a world matching that description, biological samples might shed more light on what kind of being we're dealing with."

Kira exchanged glances with her team members. "Sir, none of us are trained botanists."

Sandren smiled. "Considering your skillset includes hacking into complex computer systems while under enemy fire, we figured picking flowers would be within your ability level."

Kira smiled back. "So long as you don't require an aesthetically balanced bouquet in a vase, sir, we should be able to manage."

"Hey now," Ari interjected, "I've been known to make some lovely arrangements when the situation demands."

Kaen sighed and shook his head.

"We'll keep that in mind," Kira told him. *That's very good to know.* She added the tidbit to her mental file for the practical joke payback she had been planning.

"Stand by for departure details," Sandren stated. "You're all dismissed—except Kira."

She remained seated while the rest of her team departed. "Sir?" she said when she was alone with the two officers.

Kaen folded his hands on the table. "Major Sandren and I discussed your condition while we were planning the upcoming op. After reviewing the mission report from Mysar, it appears you've gained some control over the abilities granted by your new nanites, but not enough to be reliable."

"Yes, sir," Kira acknowledged.

"We understand that Leon developed a suppressant for you, though the side effects are unknown," Kaen continued. "Frankly, we don't have time to go through proper trials to see if that's a viable solution—especially given that we don't know how the nanites are coded to you, specifically."

Kira nodded. "I agree."

"For that reason, the best option seems for you to be paired with an AI," Kaen concluded.

Kira's heart skipped a beat. "Sir?" Leon had already suggested that option to her after she returned from Mysar, but she hadn't yet given it proper consideration.

"I did. We've identified an AI on Lynaeda who seems like she'd be a perfect fit for your present situation. She received an excellent recommendation from one of Doctor Elric's colleagues."

Sharing my head with someone else... Kira took a slow breath. "Do I have time to think about it?" she asked.

"We'll need to know before we depart for Gaelon, and we can't delay that mission for long," Sandren replied. "You can have an hour."

"And if I don't want to move forward with the procedure?" Kira questioned.

"Then we'd have a discussion," Kaen stated.

They either convince me, or reevaluate my role on the mission. Kira took a slow breath. "Yes, sir, I'll let you know."

CHAPTER 2

As soon as she was dismissed, Kira sent Leon a message to meet at her quarters.

They'd had little alone time since she returned from Mysar, so the notion of heading out to Gaelon so soon didn't thrill her. However, she wouldn't rest easy until she was certain the alien threat had been neutralized. In the meantime, she could use a sounding board for the decision about getting an AI.

Leon was waiting outside her door when she arrived. "Hey," he greeted.

"Hey. You made it here fast."

"I was already on my way back from the lab." He looked her over. "You're going to Gaelon, aren't you?"

She nodded. "Order just came down."

He sighed. "All right."

Kira opened the door and stepped inside. "I feel like I just got back."

"Because you pretty much did."

"True." She grabbed her travel bag from its storage cubby and tossed it on the bed. "I swear, things normally aren't like this."

"The part about evil forces threatening to destroy the galaxy or you traveling a lot?"

Kira thought about it. "Okay, so maybe both of those things happen more often than I realized. I guess I'm just not used to *leaving* someone when I go on a mission."

Leon sat down on the edge of the bed to watch her pack. "We have plenty of time to figure things out. I had no expectations when I took this job. You have a career and a life here independent of me."

"Stars, how are you so nice and understanding?"

He raised an eyebrow. "Is that a bad thing?"

"No." She grabbed a pile of underwear from a drawer and dropped it in her bag. "You're entirely too good at being objective."

"Well, I *am* a scientist," he pointed out with heavy sarcasm.

Kira only rolled her eyes in response.

"Okay, fine, you want to know my secret?"

She paused her packing. "Please, enlighten me."

Leon propped his hands behind him on the bed. "When everything went down on Valta, my entire life was turned upside down. You came back into the picture, I realized that what I thought was my dream job was in fact a corporation controlled by evil aliens, and I discovered my sister had been intending to assassinate a president. Oh, and I watched you strangle a woman."

"Yeah, that was a thing."

"Needless to say, it was a pretty rough few days," Leon continued. "As I was processing all of it afterward, I realized that I didn't completely lose my shite while it was going down. Freaking out at any number of times during those events would have been tantamount to death, so I stuck it out. And, I survived. That got me thinking, maybe it wasn't productive to get upset about a lot of the little things that happen on a day-to-day basis."

Kira cast him a sidelong glance. "Are you suggesting that you decided to not let anything get to you when you came here?"

"Not exactly," he clarified, sitting upright. "More like, I decided from now on, every time I feel myself getting worried or angry, I ask myself if having a gut reaction will help the situation. Sometimes, that adrenaline rush is just what's needed—like when I was down on Valta getting the equipment out of the lab, and we were attacked. But getting upset when you have to go off and do your job? That doesn't help either of us. I'd rather enjoy the time we do get to spend together."

"I can totally tell that this is scientist-you applying logic to real life, but you're right."

"I feel like I should get a recording of those last two words being spoken in that order."

Kira rolled her eyes. "I admit when I'm wrong."

"You do." Leon beckoned her, and she sat down next to him on the bed. He took her hands in his. "But in this case, it's not a matter of correctness. I just don't see the point in spending energy getting upset about circumstances that won't change no matter what I do."

"I could use some more of that attitude myself. There's been a lot to come to terms with."

Leon caught her gaze. "And we can help each other with that."

She squeezed his hand and leaned her head on his shoulder. "I'm really happy to have your freaky calmness."

"Always." He kissed her forehead.

Kira pulled away. "There's something else. Before we go to

Gaelon, they want me to get an AI."

Leon's eyes widened. "An AI? That's quite a step."

"Yeah." She frowned. "I know you'd suggested it already, and there are definitely merits to a pairing. It's just a little different when it's a formal request."

"They're not forcing you, are they?"

"No, they'd never violate autonomy like that. It's more of a 'highly encourage' kind of scenario. But, if I don't want to, I could see my position on my team being reevaluated."

He searched her eyes. "How do you feel about it?"

She shrugged. "I've spent a lot of time being in other people's heads. It's strange to think of someone being in mine."

"Don't do anything that makes you uncomfortable."

"That's not my hesitation. The tech is well-established."

"Then, what?" Leon asked with concern in his voice.

Kira searched for the right words. "What if the AI discovers that the nanites have done something to me beyond what other tests have shown? I mean, they're coded to me and don't transmit to others. Does that mean they're linked to my DNA, or something?"

"Blissful ignorance doesn't solve problems."

"But it's so much less stressful!" Kira cracked a smile.

Leon squeezed her hand. "If it does discover something, then I'll do whatever I can to help you find a solution to that, too."

She sighed. "Not getting the upgrade would just be delaying the inevitable."

"I think that's the right call, for what it's worth." He eyed her. "Not to mention, you already started packing for an op you knew you likely wouldn't go on unless you get the AI."

Kira stared down at her half-packed bag. "Huh, I guess I did."

"Never underestimate the power of your subconscious."

Kira nodded. "Decided before I realized it. Well, I guess I should finish packing and then report to Medical."

"Of course. I'll just sit here and silently judge your lack of folding technique."

She gave Leon a playful shove as she walked toward her dresser, and he caught her hand on the backswing.

He drew her back to stand in front of him while he remained seated on the bed. "Look, joking aside, I know we're still figuring each other out again. We spent a decade apart, and even now you're going through some major transitions—first the nanites, and soon you'll have a new AI to get to know. As tempting as it is to pick up right where we left off, we're not the same people we were when we were a couple before."

Kira placed her hands on his shoulders. "I like the first impression of the new you as much as the old one, and I want to see where this can go."

"I'd like that, too."

She gave him a quick kiss. "But right now, I really do need to pack."

"I know. I'll leave you to it." He started to get up.

"Stay. Keep me company," she told him, resuming her packing.

Leon settled back on the bed. "Do you think you'll find that world you saw in your vision?"

Kira glanced at him over her shoulder. "If we do, I'm worried what might be on the surface."

"It goes without saying, but be careful."

"I will."

— — —

Rebuilding the Mysaran government was proving even more difficult than it sounded on paper, and Ellen Calleti had anticipated it would be anything but straightforward. As she reviewed the latest report about the government officials who had been under alien telepathic influence, she was reminded just how large the job ahead would be.

Ellen sighed and spun around in her office chair to look out the window at the Elusian capital city. *I'll never be able to take care of everything from here.*

Mid-morning sun bathed the glass buildings in a warm glow. The city had become her home, despite the roundabout way she'd come to serve the world. Even with her continued ties to Mysar and Valta, her first duty going forward had to be to Elusia.

In that capacity, it was critical that she help restore stability to the Elvar Trinary. Following the Mysaran chancellor's untimely death, the power vacuum had introduced opportunity for the wrong people to force their way to the top. President Joris of Elusia was counting on her to make sure that didn't happen. But sitting in an office a world away didn't provide a great deal of control.

Ellen rose from her desk. *I know what I have to do, but going back there...*

Mysar had become a place of bad memories. Her years in school during her early-twenties had been what any young person would wish for, but her involvement in the dark dealings of the subverted Mysaran government, and its secret manipulations of the Sovereign activists, had forever changed her impressions of the world. Even though this was her opportunity to rebuild, part of her was afraid of how much more unpleasantness would be uncovered and further taint what few positive memories she did have of Mysar.

"Worrying about what I *might* find won't help anyone," she muttered to herself.

With a heavy sigh, she trudged to the door.

President Joris' office was two floors above her own. The elevator deposited her in the reception area.

Behind the reception desk, Nico smiled at her. "Finally decided you need to go in person?" the young man asked.

Ellen tilted her head. "How did you know?"

"Based on the recent communications regarding Mysar, it doesn't take much extrapolation."

"Good point. Is Joris free?"

"Should be wrapping up a call any minute," Nico replied. "I'll let you know."

Ellen took a seat in one of the waiting chairs at the center of the lobby, using the time to create a mental packing list for her upcoming journey. She'd have to dig through her closet for some lighter-weight dress clothes, for sure.

After five minutes, Nico gave her the go-ahead to enter the president's office.

"Good morning, sir," Ellen greeted as she opened the door.

"How are you doing, Ellen?" President Joris was standing behind his desk while reading from a tablet. He glanced up when she approached the desk.

"Fine, sir. I've reviewed the present state of affairs on Mysar, and I think it's prudent for me to go in person."

He nodded. "I thought that might eventually be the case."

She smiled. "It seems like since I officially became your press secretary, I've done almost everything *but* that job."

"I think you've written a speech or two," Joris replied with a smirk.

"Well, I do need to justify my employment." She chuckled. "At any rate, I'd like to go to Mysar so I can really dig into things."

"I anticipated that when I suggested you work on this. It's what we need to solidify the relationship with the new leadership, whoever that may be."

"More than that, I'm hoping to do some recon," Ellen continued.

"Regarding what?"

"The ancillary government activities. I've seen a handful of reports containing conflicting information about production, with no clear trail for where the materials went."

Joris gave her a questioning look. "Trade with Elusia and Valta?"

"Not enough to account for it," she replied.

"Another question for others to answer on our behalf." Joris sat down in the swivel chair behind his desk.

Ellen raised an eyebrow and took a seat in one of the two guest chairs across from him. "Have you heard from the Guard?"

"Yes, but they've given no indication about specific action items. However, now that Colonel Kaen is himself again, I've been assured that all future matters regarding this situation will be dealt with swiftly and decisively."

"That sounds more like it."

He nodded. "Music to my ears."

"Anything else you'd like me to be on the lookout for while I'm on Mysar?" Ellen asked.

Joris turned serious. "Potential threat to us, present or

future. If the Mysarans have a secret militia stashed away somewhere, I'd rather know about it now than find out when they send a landing party to Elusia."

"Consider it done, sir."

He nodded. "Safe travels. You'll have a job waiting for you when you return."

Ellen smiled. "I won't hold my breath for it to be the same one."

— — —

Colonel Terence Kaen wasn't particularly fond of interruptions, but he couldn't ignore a call from the Elusian president. With a sigh, he activated the video call on his office viewscreen.

"Hello, Mister President, what can I do for you?"

"I'm sorry to interrupt," Joris said, smoothing back his white hair. There was a slight flush to his face, highlighting his light blue eyes. "I wanted to give you an update on our rebuilding efforts."

"Yes, I've been meaning to check in with you. How are things progressing?"

The president smiled. "Ellen is in the thick of it now. Again, I can't thank you enough for stepping in to help on Mysar before."

Kaen held back a scowl. "We would have moved in regardless. As I explained, we were only delayed in acting because of my… condition."

"Forgive me, I should have asked how you're doing."

"Good as new," Kaen replied. It was close enough to the truth to share with an acquaintance.

However, if he was being honest, it would take time to get

over his experience—the feeling of being trapped inside himself. The alien, Nox, had been able to exert a level of control that no being should have over another. Kaen had never given up, but he'd certainly seen the potential for a dark outcome that he wasn't eager to encounter again.

"Glad to hear you're well," the president continued. "I know you're busy, so I won't pester you with more pleasantries. The reason for my call is to let you know that we've reached out to Mysar to engage in political talks."

"Good, but you're not beholden to keep the Guard apprised of your activities." Kaen folded his hands on his desktop.

"Of course. I only thought it relevant to inform you because we have certain suspicions we hope to either confirm or refute through the investigation."

"Which are?"

"That Mysar had been producing more than the system used. Official records can't account for the discrepancy."

Kaen's brow furrowed. "Where do you suspect it went?"

"Toward some secret activity that the alien controlling Chancellor Hale was up to," the president replied. "If that proves to be the case, we'll need outside assistance to determine what those materials were used for and if there's an ongoing threat."

If I had to guess, that material ended up in Gaelon. Kaen nodded. "Thank you for the heads up. We'll be standing by for your findings."

"Take care." The president ended the call.

Kaen leaned back in his chair. If the aliens were building something, their supply from Mysar had now been cut off. *That might not matter if the project was already complete, or if they were just getting started. But if a project was near completion... they might be all the more aggressive to see it through to the end.*

He released a slow breath. Whatever Kira's team was up against, it was going to be a revealing expedition.

CHAPTER 3

KIRA FIDGETED ON her exam bed. She'd been prepped with various injections over the past day to make her body receptive to the upcoming AI hardware installation. All that remained was to meet her intended AI partner and confirm that they were both willing to proceed with the pairing procedure.

Normally, a soldier and AI would spend weeks getting to know each other, but Guard Command had been insistent about an accelerated timeline. In the interest of expediency, Kira had begun the physical preparations while the AI, Jasmine, was transferred from a Guard base near Lynaeda.

"Jasmine has just arrived on the base's local Net. Are you ready to meet?" Doctor Elric asked Kira, coming to stand next to the exam bed.

"Can't wait," Kira said, far more nervous than she could recall being for any other meeting.

Elric handed her a headset. "A voice chat will be different than the direct neural link of a pairing, but it will give you a chance to feel each other out."

Kira put in the earbud and pointed the integrated

microphone toward her mouth. "Okay."

"Patching you into a meeting space now." The doctor left her alone in the private room.

"Hello, Kira," a warm, slightly synthesized-sounding female voice greeted.

"Hi. You must be Jasmine."

"I am."

Kira tried to get comfortable on the bed. "That's an unusual AI name, isn't it? I'd heard a lot of you adopt acronyms for your designation."

"Yes, that is tradition—such as the CACI clones found throughout the branches of the Taran military. In my case, one of my early fascinations was with botany. I always found jasmine flowers particularly beautiful, so I took it as my name."

"It's a nice choice." Kira paused. "Hey, as much as I'd like some getting-to-know-you small-talk, I think we should cut to the chase. Have they told you about me—you know, about the Robus nanites?"

"I appreciate your directness. Yes, I was given your official file and the relevant reports related to MTech's research," Jasmine confirmed. "It was actually because of your unique situation that I was interested in the pairing."

"I don't know if *I'd* risk being paired with me."

"You risk your wellbeing whenever you depart on an op, do you not?"

"Yes, of course," Kira replied. "But that's to help others."

"It's no different for me. You are in a difficult position, and I believe I can help you—in addition to helping those you would aid through your own actions, by extension."

Kira swallowed. "Admittedly, I could use someone I trust to have my back. I love my team, but they don't fully understand what's going on with me."

"I would like that opportunity," Jasmine said.

"Have you been paired with a person before?" Kira asked.

"Yes, on two prior occasions. You would be the first soldier, however."

The revelation caught Kira by surprise. She had figured they'd partner her with an AI specializing in covert operations to match her own skillset. "What did you do before?" Kira asked.

"My specialization is in biomedical research."

"Ah, so *that's* why they thought we'd be a good match."

"I am excited to learn more about your abilities," Jasmine said.

Kira looked down. "I'll be honest, Jasmine. You seem friendly, and certainly knowledgeable, but I don't see how we could possibly get to know each other on any deep level in the next few minutes."

"I agree, Kira. This is a big decision for both of us—for you, especially, since it would be your first pairing. I would never want you to feel rushed, but the present circumstances don't allow for standard vetting."

"Yeah, that's been made clear."

"From my side," Jasmine continued, "I have reviewed the facts regarding the aliens, and my assessment is that you are the Guard's best chance to interface with whatever may be in Gaelon. I believe I can help you safely complete that mission, so I am willing to try this pairing if you are."

Kira smiled. "A spur-of-the-moment AI pairing wouldn't be the most surprising thing that's happened to me in the last two weeks."

"You really have had quite the month."

"If you're willing to move forward knowing all of that, then who am I to say 'no'?" Kira took a deep breath. "Okay, let's do this."

"I'm glad to hear that, Kira," Jasmine said. "I look forward to getting properly acquainted after I'm embedded in the deepest recesses of your mind and there's no going back."

"Um…"

"I'm joking, Kira! I may not be organic, but I do have a sense of humor."

Kira laughed. "Well played. The test remains if you'll be able to withstand my unmitigated snark."

"Challenge accepted."

Kira's anxiety from before the introduction began to dissipate. Jasmine would still be a stranger inside her head, but she could see them becoming good friends in time. "All right, I guess I'll see you on the other side. Or… inside?"

"Something like that. Try to relax."

"I'm feeling better already." Kira removed the headset and then poked her head out of the room. She spotted Doctor Elric at a nearby workstation. "Doctor, we're agreed," she told him. "Let's move forward with the pairing."

The doctor returned to her exam room. "That wasn't a very long talk."

"That's all we needed."

"Very well. I'll make the final preparations." Elric turned his attention to the medpod in the room, where the surgery would take place. The device looked entirely too simple from the outside, considering everything it could do.

Kira took a calming breath while she waited for Doctor Elric's instructions. *I'm still going to be me. Jasmine will be someone to talk to when I'm bored.* Though she was trying to be light-hearted about it, the reality was that having a constant companion in her mind would be a huge change, standard procedure or not. She'd still have private thoughts, but not like she could before. She hoped Jasmine would respect those boundaries.

"Okay, all set," Elric said. He beckoned Kira over.

"Will it hurt?" she asked, approaching the pod.

"A little discomfort is to be expected, considering you'll be cut open and fitted with new augmentations."

Kira paled. "I guess I hadn't thought about that part."

"Don't dwell on it. The incision sites will be fully closed by the time you wake up. You can expect your nerves to be over-reactive for a bit afterward, but I know for a fact that you've been through much worse."

"I'm sure I can handle it," Kira said.

"The procedure will only take about two hours," Doctor Elric explained. "We'll install a communication chip in your brain for the AI interface before we begin the pairing. The main AI hardware installation will begin inside your rib cage, followed by the hardwire connection along your spinal column to the neural communication chip. The AI consciousness will then be transferred to your new hardware. Finally, you'll get a dose of specialized med-nano to aid the AI in evaluating your physiological state and make sure there won't be any conflicts with your Robus nanites—think of it as a super-charged version of your standard immune support nanotech."

Kira's eyes widened. "All that in two hours?"

"It's an efficient system," he assured her. "Are you ready?" She nodded.

"Please undress and climb inside."

Kira took a deep breath in a vain attempt to calm her lingering nerves and began stripping down. Once naked, she quickly climbed into the medpod to avoid standing on the cold tile.

As she reclined inside, the space seemed much more like a coffin than a sophisticated medical device. *What am I so worried about? This is a standard procedure in other parts of the*

Empire. She focused on her breathing.

The medpod's lid sealed her inside.

"Stay still and try to breathe normally," Doctor Elric said over an internal comm. "You may feel a tingle as you start to go under."

Kira did as she was instructed. She felt a tickle along her spine as her eyelids grew heavy. Calm darkness enveloped her.

When the medpod's lid popped open, it didn't feel like more than a minute had passed.

"Take it slow," Elric said, coming to stand over her. "How do you feel?"

"Fine—" Kira started to reply but cut off as soon as she tried to sit up. Sharp pain stabbed her head and radiated along her spine. "Gah!"

The doctor placed a hand on her bare shoulder, urging her to lay back down. "Your nerves were just reknitted. The sensitivity will subside within an hour."

Kira remained motionless for several minutes, giving her senses time to adjust. *I thought I'd feel more different. Where is—*

<I didn't want to intrude.> Kira recognized Jasmine's voice in her mind even though she wasn't hearing it with her ears this time.

Whoa! Kira's pulse spiked with the sudden appearance of the mental presence.

<I'm sorry, I didn't mean to alarm you.>

<No, it's fine,> Kira replied, trying to parse out the difference between her private thoughts and the internal speech. *<Sorry, this is weird.>*

<I know. You can get up now.>

Kira realized she was still reclined in the medpod. *<Right, yes.>*

She tried to sit up again, slower this time. The initial physical discomfort she'd experienced had faded to a dull ache in her neck and back. She climbed out of the device.

Doctor Elric handed her the shipsuit and undergarments she'd removed before the procedure. "I'll let you get dressed." He departed.

Kira began donning her clothes. <Can you read all my thoughts?> she asked Jasmine in her mind.

The AI chuckled—an odd sensation behind Kira's eyes that almost made her feel like she had to sneeze. <I can only see what you want to share with me. You are far more proficient with the distinction than most.>

<The telepath thing, I guess.>

<It's a rare skill. I have never experienced such a mind before,> Jasmine said. <It will take me some time to get used to your body, but I have every belief that this will be a rewarding partnership.>

<Me too. I don't much care for the idea that I could randomly transform.>

<I hope I'll be able to help you with that,> Jasmine told her.

<I do, too.> Kira finished dressing in her shipsuit and then left the exam room. She found Doctor Elric talking to a nurse.

Elric dismissed the nurse. "Feeling better?" he asked Kira.

"Yes. Jasmine and I have been getting to know each other better."

"Ah, good." The doctor smiled. "Any lingering pain?"

"Not too bad. That first jolt was the worst."

He nodded. "It should all be gone soon. Jasmine will be able to help with future pain regulation, once you two finish syncing."

"I'm more interested to see how she deals with my impulsiveness," Kira replied.

<I think I'll manage.> Jasmine gave a mental nod—a far less disorienting sensation than a laugh.

<You say that now, but just wait until we're running from the bad guys while they're trying to blow us up.>

<Admittedly, that sounds stressful.>

<Yeah, that's one way to put it, Kira responded with a mental chuckle. *<But don't worry, you get used to being shot at.>*

<Hmm.>

Kira laughed out loud.

Doctor Elric gave her a quizzical look.

"Poor Jasmine is coming to terms with the insanity that is my life," Kira explained.

"Ah." The doctor nodded. "Good luck with that."

<Jasmine, do I need to remain under observation and recover or am I good to go?> Kira asked her new AI friend.

<The pairing is complete and your body is responding well. I see no reason for you to remain here.>

"Is there anything else, Doctor?" Kira asked Elric. "I'd like to let Major Sandren know I'm ready for the mission."

Elric nodded. "I've gone over your post-pairing scans, and everything looks to be in order. I'll clear you for duty, but come in for a check-up when you return from Gaelon."

"Yes, Doctor. See you then."

Kira headed for the interface terminal outside of Medical so she could send Sandren a message.

<You know, now that you have me, you don't need a console to send messages,> Jasmine said.

<Then how?>

<I'm linked into the local Net, of course. We're a team. I can send communications on your behalf.>

Kira smiled. *<Now* that *will be handy.>*

Jasmine sent a copy of Kira's medical clearance to Major

Sandren, and an acknowledgement soon came back that the *Raven* would depart for Gaelon in half an hour.

Kira headed to her quarters to retrieve her travel bag. While she was there, she also wanted to let Leon know the procedure had gone off without trouble; that kind of personal communication didn't feel right to be relayed by Jasmine.

>>Paring complete!<< she wrote Leon. >>I'm officially a 'tech head'. Departing for Gaelon now.<<

He took a moment to message back. >>Do you have time for a proper goodbye?<<

>>No, but I'll see you soon. Try to stay out of trouble.<<

>>You, too. Be careful, Kira.<<

>>Always.<<

She grabbed her travel bag from next to the door and headed out.

As she made the trek from the residential area to the docking location of the *Raven*, Kira could sense Jasmine's fascination of seeing sights for the first time that had become commonplace to Kira after so many years.

<This is nothing. Wait until we're in the heat of battle,> Kira said.

<But you're covert ops.>

Kira thought she detected a hint of concern in the AI's mental tone. *<You're out of the research lab now, Jasmine! Welcome to the Tararian Guard.>*

<Perhaps my preliminary evaluation of this pairing neglected to take into account some of the variables involved in your field activities.>

<Having second thoughts?> Kira asked.

<No, just updating the assumptions in my statistical calculations for the likelihood of us ending up as a smear on the deck.>

<Am I doomed?>

<My estimations show that eventuality to be highly unlikely,> Jasmine replied. *<We might be stuck with each other for a while.>*

<Glad to know I'm not a completely disastrous mess.>

<No, not completely. Just... 'mess prone'.>

Kira smirked. *<Yes, we'll go with that.>*

She arrived at the *Raven* and used the gangway to board the craft. It deposited her on the residential level, and she walked down the short hall to the cabin she shared with her team.

The other soldiers were unpacking their travel bags when Kira opened the door.

"Hey," Kira greeted them.

"Is it done?" Nia asked.

Kira nodded. She set down her bag on her bunk in the lower left of the room. "Yep. I'd like to introduce you to Jasmine."

The AI connected to the comm system inside the cabin. "Pleasure to meet you," Jasmine greeted.

"You're in for quite a ride," Kyle replied.

"It's only been a few minutes since our pairing, but I've gotten that distinct impression," the AI said.

"It'll be nice finally having an AI on the team," Nia added. "Sometimes it would be nice to have extra help with the hacks."

"Really?" Kyle shook his head. "I've always liked going it alone. I live for the challenge."

"A partnership doesn't diminish your individual abilities," Jasmine pointed out over the comm.

"No offense meant," Kyle hastily amended.

"None taken. I know that not everyone enjoys a pairing. I will strive to be a productive member of your team, in whatever capacity will be mutually beneficial."

<You sure you didn't work as a diplomat?> Kira mentally asked the AI.

<Just because I'm scientifically minded, that doesn't mean I can't have good social skills, too,> Jasmine replied with a mental wink.

"If you can help keep Kira from transforming into a Robus against her will, I'm happy to have you along," Ari said.

"We can use the transit time to get synced," Jasmine suggested. "I have reviewed all of Kira's medical records, and I have some ideas for how to regulate the transformation."

"Sounds good to me," Kira agreed. *<I'm very curious to see how this works,>* she added privately.

<Me too.>

<It'll be some real hands-on study, that's for sure.> Kira returned her attention to her teammates. "Now that introductions are out of the way, I think we need to address something that no one has wanted to say aloud."

Each of the soldiers sat down on their respective bunks.

"We're up against something entirely new here," Kira began when everyone was situated. "What we witnessed with Colonel Kaen and Chancellor Hale was only one facet of this race's capabilities. We know they can take over people with a compatible TR, but they have also swayed a number of individuals to work with them of their own free will. The ability to be so persuasive suggests a high level of social awareness that is contrary to Kaen's experience with Nox."

"Yeah, it sounded like Nox was *really* bad at blending in, once it asserted itself," Kyle agreed.

"A clear distinction," Kira confirmed. "When I talked to Nox, it seemed annoyed with our social constructs. Yet, Reya was adept at working within those systems to build what appears to be an elaborate distribution system throughout the Elvar Trinary, and maybe beyond."

"People each possess different skillsets," Nia pointed out. "It's not unreasonable to assume that the Gaelons, or whatever we want to call them, would have variation in their individual proclivities, as well."

Kira nodded. "You're absolutely right. Where I'm going with this is that we're working with a sample size of *two* right now. We have no idea what other variations there are—how strong they might be or how good at manipulating—but they're *smart*. Monica didn't come up with the alien hybrid nanites on her own; she was using information that the Gaelons relayed to her." She paused. "You know, we really need a better name for these guys."

"It's not suitably evil-sounding," Nia agreed.

"Their actions may appear evil from our vantage, but who's to say this isn't a cultural misunderstanding?" Kyle countered. "I'm not sure it's fair to paint them squarely as the bad guys."

"Remember what they did to Hale, making her a prisoner in her own mind for *decades*?" Kira pointed out.

Kyle held up his hands. "I retract my statement. Evil-sounding name, it is."

"Gaels?" Ari suggested, but he immediately scrunched up his nose and shook his head.

"Lons, maybe?" Nia ventured.

"Still doesn't have a good ring to it," Kyle said. "Maybe trying to pull in the system name isn't the right way to go. Perhaps something having to do with their traits instead?"

Kira nodded. "They whisper in people's minds, try to control them."

"The 'Whispers', or 'Controllers'…" Ari shook his head.

"No, that's not right."

"What about 'Trol', short for 'control'?" Kyle suggested.

Nia tilted her head. "Too on point?"

Kira considered it. "You know, it does have that 'mysterious baddie' quality to it. I like it."

"Watch, they'll declare they have their own name that's something terrible, like the Fooferies," Ari said through an amused snort.

"Stars! And then we'd have to use the official designation." Kira groaned. "Let's hit it hard with 'Trols' now, while we can, and hope it sticks."

"I'm for it," Kyle agreed, followed by Nia and Ari voicing their support.

<Wow, I cannot believe that discussion just happened,> Jasmine interjected privately.

<Hey, at least this one was on topic. Wait until Ari goes off on a tangent about one of his videos.>

<Speaking of which, you're quite a gifted dancer.>

<Oh, foknuggets. You saw that?>

<Of course. It was the most viewed video in multiple categories. I deemed it appropriate research to prepare for our pairing.>

Kira was silent for a moment. *<Jasmine, you're messing with me, aren't you?>*

<I couldn't resist.>

Her AI did, indeed, have a jokester streak. *I better keep Jasmine in my good graces or Ari will have a source with access to way too much material.*

Considerations for another time.

"The point is," Kira said, trying to get back on topic, "now more than ever, we'll need to have each other's backs."

"How do we attack an enemy we can't see?" Ari asked,

always seeming to think with his gun.

Kira smiled at the huge soldier. "They have a physical presence, even if it's something different than what we're used to. We'll find what it is and figure out how to disable them."

"Not destroy?" Kyle questioned.

"That's not for us to decide at this juncture," Kira replied. "We're investigating a new lifeform. It's not right to take the fate of a race lightly, even though they did paint a giant target on their telepathic backs."

Nia eyed her. "And if our investigation confirms everything we already suspect about them?"

Kira's hazel eyes took on a slight orange cast for a moment. "Then their last thoughts will be regrets for ever messing with my home."

CHAPTER 4

WITH KIRA BUSY in the Gaelon System for at least the next three days, Leon returned his attention to the tests looking for TRs in Guard personnel.

He settled into his workstation in his lab with coffee in hand. *What awesomeness awaits me today?*

Working with Doctor Elric, Leon and his team had developed an automated process to compare historical medical records with a new scan, but like any batch processing system, it was imperfect. The system kicked back the occasional inconclusive result, which required manual review.

Though Leon's graduate degree was in genetics—he'd made that very clear—the rest of the team had spun his credentials to insist that that also made him an expert in neuroscience, and therefore he was the best person to review each and every one of those inconclusive records. While he could easily have pushed back and assigned the project to Tess or Jack, he decided to give them a pass this time around and just do it himself. A happy team was a productive team, and he'd rather have a favor stashed in the bank.

As he did his morning inventory of the test results on his dashboard, Leon was happy to see fewer files to review than he'd feared.

"Hello!" Tess greeted as she entered the lab, pulling Leon's attention from the screen.

"Hey."

"Why the grumpy tone?" she asked while sitting down at her own station across the room. The workspace was affixed with an odd assortment of a dozen magnetic stickers, including a cat wearing a spacesuit and a taco with rocket engines that Leon hadn't noticed before.

How can she work like that? Leon shook his head. "The system is still kicking back these 'inconclusive' results," he replied. "I'm getting sick of the manual review."

"Is there any common factor with those records?" Tess placed her hand on the desktop to log into the workstation. "Maybe we can tweak the analysis algorithm."

Leon took another sip of coffee. "I don't think I'm awake enough for that yet."

"Get to it, boss! We have a lot to do today." Tess grinned. She turned her attention to her screen and brought up her inbox.

"Wow, do you always have this much energy first thing in the morning?" Leon asked.

She glanced over her shoulder at him with a raised eyebrow. "It's 10:00. I've already had two meetings today."

"Is it?" He checked the time on his dashboard. "Guess I got a late start."

"I'll say."

Leon turned back to his work. *At least my team is more responsible with time management than I am.*

Tess was silent for a moment, tapping her finger on the

desk. "Wait, where's Jack?"

"Elric wanted him for something," Leon responded without taking his eyes off his monitor. He took a deep breath. *Is she ever going to break that habit of tapping while she thinks?*

Tess was silent for another thirty seconds as she continued tapping her finger. She stopped. "Oh, that explains it."

"Hmm?"

"Why didn't you tell me Kira got an AI?"

Leon swiveled his stool to face her. "Why is that relevant?"

Tess sighed and folded her hands in her lap. "Because Jack's specialty is in bioelectronics integrations. We got thrown together on this team when you arrived, and we've been sort of fielding the random requests that have come in. But now that we don't have an immediate crisis on our hands, this is an opportunity to take an approach that caters to our specialties."

"And that's connected to Kira... how?"

"Now that she has an AI, we can figure out what's going on with her," Tess stated.

Leon crossed his arms. "She has an alien strain of nanites. I've run the genetic models. We already know what changes they've made to her."

Tess nodded. "On the physical level, yes. But now we have a chance to learn about how the tech *thinks*."

"I didn't get the impression that the nanites are a sentient entity."

"No, not like that," his assistant replied with a touch of annoyance in her tone. "I mean, like, how it operates based on the specific circumstances. We know *what* it does, but her transformations have been random. With the detailed data her AI will collect, we'll be able to analyze the specific conditions at the moment she's about to transform—the triggers and the variables that impact the speed and expression of her abilities."

All right, so she knows her stuff. Leon leaned against his stool's backrest. "I hadn't thought about that part."

Tess pursed her lips with a hint of smugness. "It's easy to think of the AI as just being a regulator, but for it to do that job, it needs to perform that analysis. We can access that data and learn even more about the nanotech."

"What can we do with that information?" he prompted.

"Well, if we understand the triggers, we might be able to glean some more insights into what the aliens were after when they designed the tech."

Leon perked up. "Stars! I didn't think of that. The trigger points will indicate certain expectations for the physiological state the Robus would be in. How they'd be used."

"Precisely." She held up her index finger victoriously.

"Except, we already know the plan was to turn them into soldiers."

"Yes," Tess acknowledged, "but if we know the chemical threshold to trigger a transformation, it'll indicate how long one could stay in that state."

"Blitz fights or extended conflicts," he said.

"You've got it."

"Huh." Leon nodded, impressed by her reasoning. "So, what might Jack be doing with Doctor Elric?"

"Probably figuring out a way to port the medical monitoring into our models of the nanotech expression so we can get a holistic view."

He chuckled. "You were doing just fine on your own before I came along, weren't you?"

She smiled. "We didn't have the genetics angle before. It's great to have you on the team now."

"Glad I'm not completely useless!"

"No way." Tess flipped her wrist. "Besides, it's not just

anyone who'd volunteer to go through all those records."

Leon laughed. "There's grunt work with any job."

"You're in charge, but you took that task on yourself. Don't think we didn't notice."

"I appreciate that."

She nodded. "Sure thing."

"Well, I should get back to this," Leon said, glancing back at his screen.

"Have fun." Tess smirked.

"Yeah, and you with your… whatever you're doing." *Guess that's not very good management if I have no idea what my team is working on, whoops.* He made a mental note to get caught up on their side projects and specialties so he'd be able to delegate more effectively in the future.

"I will," Tess said, offering no further insight into what her current project may be. "Oh, but first, there is one more thing."

"Sure, what?"

The young scientist shifted in her seat. "I know we have things under control here in the Guard, but what kind of testing is happening on Mysar?"

Leon nodded. "I was thinking about that, too. Even though we gave them our algorithm and the procedures, we have no way of knowing if they're following those protocols."

"Or who's reviewing the inconclusive results," Tess added.

"There's not a lot we can do about it."

"Isn't it our responsibility to make sure this is done right?"

Leon shrugged. "Not particularly. Mysar isn't even an Empire world."

Tess tilted her head and raised an eyebrow. "Was that supposed to sound convincing?"

He chuckled. "All right, I spent way too much time on Mysar to not care about what happens there."

"Not to mention, now that the government is in transition, it's not unlikely that they'll be joining the Empire soon."

"Yeah, it doesn't make sense for Elusia to be in and not have Mysar and Valta in, as well," Leon replied. Not too long ago, he would have thought unity among the three worlds was only an aspirational, distant future. To now have that reality so close at hand still caught him by surprise.

"Right." Tess nodded. "And given that eventuality, we need to make sure there aren't any threats to the Taran Empire once we start mixing together." She waggled her fingers, as though kneading dough.

"I don't have any suggestions for how to improve the oversight."

Tess smiled. "But I bet you do know who would."

— — —

Compared to her last visit, Ellen's nerves were considerably more settled as her shuttle came to rest on the landing pad outside one of Mysar's many biodomes. At last, she was returning to the planet as her real self, not some fictionalized modern version of her twisted past.

She gazed out the viewport at the nearest translucent dome glimmering under the early-afternoon sun. Interlocking triangular panels formed the enclosure for the three-kilometer-wide dome, which was one of five connected structures comprising the city. It was the metropolis closest to the Mysaran government building from which Chancellor Hale had governed, and the place where Ellen had spent much of her time when she had lived on the world in years past.

That feels like a lifetime ago.

Her motivations and her way of thinking had been

drastically different back then. She'd thought that keeping the Elvar Trinary isolated was the best way forward. Now, she couldn't wait to help bring Mysar and Valta into the Taran Empire and solidify their partnerships with Elusia.

Ellen rose from the passenger seat on the shuttle and gathered her belongings from an overhead bin.

"Business or pleasure?" a middle-aged man asked her while he got down his own bag across the aisle.

"Business. I don't think there's a lot of tourism on Mysar," Ellen replied.

"Pleasure doesn't have to be tourism. Lots of good bars here."

Ellen cracked a smile. "Fair point."

"Are you government or private sector?" he questioned.

"Government," she told him, hoping that would be the end of the inquiries. While it wasn't a secret that she was on Mysar, it wasn't common knowledge, either. Given the complication of Elusia being in the Empire and Mysar still being on the outside, it was better if her activities on the foreign world remained behind the scenes.

"Ah." He bobbed his head of shaggy, graying hair. "Politicians. Can't live with them… and we'd probably do just fine without them."

"Fortunately for you, I'm not a politician."

"One of the poor cogs that keeps society rolling, then?"

Ellen nodded. "Someone has to do it."

"There is that." He extended the handle on his rolling bag. "Hope it's a productive meeting."

"Thank you, I'm sure it will be." She gave him a parting smile and they made their way off the shuttle with the other passengers.

At the bottom of the ramp, Ellen peered around the port

for her escort. She had been instructed that one of the government aides would meet her and take her to the government office in town. When no one was readily apparent, she headed for the main terminal, a one-story structure constructed of the dark stone common across the planet.

She was sweating by the end of the short walk. The ambient temperature was well above comfortable levels, due to the planet's proximity to the sun. While the open air was technically habitable, only life inside the biodomes felt civilized.

Ellen was about to step inside the port terminal when a woman's voice stopped her.

"Ellen Calleti?"

She turned around to identify the speaker, her gaze settling on an attractive, dark-haired woman close to her age. "Yes, hello."

"Trisha Mercer," the woman introduced.

"Thank you for coming to meet me."

"My pleasure. It was no trouble at all."

They walked away from the port to a transit station at the edge of the dome. A set of automatic doors parted and they stepped inside.

Ellen breathed in the conditioned air.

Trisha noticed her relief. "Acclimated to Elusia now?"

"Didn't think it would happen, but I have." Ellen smiled.

"It's a wonder the worlds aren't more different, given their placements," the other woman commented. "I'd expect Elusia to be a solid ball of ice."

"A lot of it is. I sometimes wonder if some ancient race prepared this system for habitation."

"And had it perfectly suited for Tarans? Doubtful, but you never know."

Ellen shrugged. "It's not so unreasonable. Our environmental tolerances mirror the state of liquid water, and that is the foundation for much of life as we know it."

"When you look at it that way, different species aren't all that dissimilar."

"At least not when it comes to what we need to survive."

The two women arrived at the maglev train terminal inside the dome. Three distinct lines snaked through the five domes, and two other tracks routed through underground tunnels, which connected to other cities over two hundred kilometers away.

Trisha directed Ellen to the main transit line. "You probably remember the government offices," she commented.

Ellen nodded. "I could never forget. Many formative years were spent hunched over a workstation there."

They boarded the train bound for the urban core at the center of the main dome. Sets of two seats facing each other in groupings of four were positioned along either side of a central aisle. Only half a dozen other people from the shuttle were boarding the train, so the two women were able to select seating with relative privacy.

"It means a lot that you came to help," Trisha said in a low voice when they sat down in their own row. "We've been a little short-staffed since the… incident."

"I can only imagine."

Trisha sat in silence for several seconds, staring absently out the window. The train began gliding forward, and she came to attention. "A lot of people won't talk about what happened."

Ellen glanced around to make sure no one was nearby. It looked private, but she knew sound could easily carry on the train. "We can talk openly once we're at the office."

The other woman nodded and resumed staring out the window.

Four-story residential buildings sped by while the train

traversed the track. The domes, numerically designated Dome 1 through 5, were each arranged with residential sectors at the perimeter and a commercial district in the center. Dome 1, at the center of the five, was almost exclusively dedicated to commercial and business functions, and it also served as the unofficial seat of the Mysaran government.

Real power had always been wielded from the official capitol building, outside the city, but few were willing to make the commute on a daily basis. Ellen now understood that had all been by design. So long as the government activities were handled in an out-of-the-way place, no one would pay much attention to the goings on. Hale, and her associates who'd been forced into servitude, had done the aliens' bidding, while the more public-facing workers in the city carried out their delegations, blissfully unaware of what was happening behind the scenes.

Ellen could only imagine what those workers were feeling now, knowing what they had been a part of. Well, she *did* know what that was like—she had been manipulated herself. And it made her feel like it would take a lifetime to make up for what she'd done.

She could see the discomfort written on Trisha's face. Ellen's heart went out to her, understanding all too well how disorienting it could be to realize that so many assumptions had been wrong.

"You shouldn't feel bad," Ellen said to break the silence. "No one knew."

As Ellen suspected, even out of context, Trisha needed no explanation. An experience so profound was ever-present on the mind. "We should have."

"Worrying about what might have been won't change anything."

Trisha took a slow breath. "I know. Like you said, we'll talk once we're at the office."

The train finished the route through the outer dome, stopping every half-kilometer, and then it passed through a translucent tunnel into the central enclosure. Buildings in the central dome were taller and more ornate, though Ellen had never understood why resources had been devoted to the enhanced aesthetics. The glass-clad structures were a waste, as far as she was concerned.

She caught herself.

Shite, I guess I should have been on the Finance Committee. It never occurred to me how much I cared. With a chuckle, she realized that her parting statement to Joris might not have been so facetious after all—her job was likely going to transition yet again.

Trisha gave her a quizzical look.

"Nothing," Ellen said with a shake of her head. "Just had a revelation about myself."

"Sounds better than my recent realizations."

"That's to be determined."

A minute later, the train glided to a smooth halt, and the two women exited.

The business district was like Ellen remembered, with workers dressed in tailored clothes, a multitude of restaurants and shops at street level, and more pedestrian traffic than seemed possible for a city of that size. She took in the sights with a smile, remembering how it had felt to be among that activity as an energetic youth.

Things could have gone so differently for me. I wonder where I would have ended up if I hadn't fallen in with the Sovereign?

She had no more time for reflection, as Trisha set out through the crowd toward one of the medium-height glass towers two blocks from the train stop.

The government building was appropriately simplistic compared to the private sector structures, but it was still at aesthetic odds with the harsh Mysaran landscape outside the dome. Rising twelve stories, it was half the height of its MTech neighbor. Seeing the proximity of the two structures, Ellen now found it to be no wonder that the line between government and private industry had blurred over the years.

Trisha led her to a conference room on the eighth floor of the government building with seating for six and a view of a rooftop park across the street.

"Now you can be honest," Ellen said as soon as the door was closed.

Trisha wilted. "I can't trust myself."

Being misled did have the tendency to make one question one's sense of identity and judgment. Ellen had recently been through that exercise herself, though it was difficult to know what to say to help the other woman without sounding trite.

"A subversion of this scale goes beyond any one person's responsibility. It's important to remember you aren't alone now," Ellen said in an attempt to console her.

Trisha shook her head, her face paling. "I still can't believe what I did."

Ellen's chest constricted. "You were one of the people who…?"

The other woman swallowed. "It's strange. I can remember everything, but it's like it was all a dream. Not a constant awareness, but looking back, I know when I was under its control and when I wasn't. But it all seemed like the same state at the time. I didn't question my actions then, but doing those same things now would make me sick."

"I've been through a good deal of that myself. These aren't

situations we can expect to get over with a moment's notice, but we can rebuild by working together."

Trisha took a shaky breath and then nodded. "Yes, you're right. And that's why we asked you here."

Ellen smiled in an attempt to set her at ease. "In all fairness, I sort of invited myself along."

The other woman chuckled. "You know, come to think of it, I guess we never *did* officially invite you."

"The long and short of it is, we're neighbors and we should try to get along better than we have in the past. I wanted to come here to begin a new friendship that can carry our nations into the future."

Trisha perked up. "We haven't taken a formal vote or anything, but based on what I've seen, I think that sentiment is shared by most of those here on Mysar."

"Good. Let's dive in."

CHAPTER 5

MISSIONS ON THE *Raven* had started to run together for Kira. The same quarters, the same people, often a similar objective. She didn't mind the repetition, but it made it difficult to remember the timing of specific experiences.

At least, that was how it had always been. As Kira wandered toward the *Raven*'s galley for an early lunch while the rest of her team napped, she was struck with a barrage of memories.

A salient recollection of her second mission with her team came to the forefront—a rather mundane experience in the context of her Guard career, but a pivotal time in the friendship between the four members of the team. Ari had spliced together different words spoken during the op to form phrases he found hilarious. Kira had no idea at the time that it was a preview of things to come.

Wow, I haven't thought about that in years. She shook her head.

<*Sorry, that may happen now and then while I get things sorted out,*> Jasmine chimed in.

<Apparently, I also need to work on keeping private thoughts separate.>

<Sorry about that, too. I'm still getting situated in here.>

<Ah.> Kira continued down the ship's central hallway toward the galley.

<I'm not trying to dig, but the way your organic memories are stored is so fascinating. Sometimes I can't help tugging on a thread that seems intriguing.>

<Glad my life history offers an interesting entertainment catalog for you,> Kira replied with what she hoped was a sarcastic mental tone.

<No need to get defensive. Whatever I observe will stay between us.>

Kira paused three meters from the galley's entry. *<Except what you need to share with the medical team.>*

Jasmine hesitated—only a split second, but that was an eternity for an AI. *<I'm not here as your overseer. We're partners.>*

<If we're partners, then we can be honest about what this is.>

<You don't want me here?>

It was Kira's turn to hesitate. *<It's not that. And it's certainly nothing against you personally. I've seen the dark side of what it's like to be in another's mind, and I'm… cautious.>*

Jasmine smiled in her mind. *<I understand, Kira. I'm not here to intrude.>*

<I also don't want you to feel like you're taking a back seat. This is my problem to get over, not yours.>

<It's only been an hour. If you had already acclimated to the pairing, I'd be concerned.>

<Fair point.>

<You'll find I have a lot of those.>

Kira smirked. *<Smug for an AI, aren't you?>*

<I am beholden to calculations. I know my worth.>

<Uh huh.> Kira covered the remaining distance to the galley.

Sven, the ship's support systems engineer, was the only occupant. Seated in the center of the table, his empty plate and half-filled glass indicated that he was at the tail end of his own meal.

"Hello, ma'am," Sven greeted with a bob of his head when he noticed her approaching.

"Please, 'Kira' is just fine while we're out here in the black," she replied. Despite knowing each other for years, they went through the same dance at the start of each mission.

He smiled. "How have you been, Kira?"

"That, my friend, is a very loaded question." She collapsed into a chair across the table from him.

"I suspected things might not be going your way when you weren't on the most recent mission to Valta."

"It's been an intense couple of weeks."

"Anything you care to share?" Sven asked.

<What's the official word on my condition?> Kira asked Jasmine.

<The Guard has not released a report on the Robus yet. Only those involved in operations on Valta are aware of the new nanotech, and only select members of Guard leadership, your team, and a handful of medical and scientific research staff are aware of your exposure.>

Kira chose her words carefully. "I've had some recent upgrades," she replied to Sven. The statement served her recent procedure in the medpod, so it seemed like a safe bet.

"Those can take getting used to."

"These are a doozy, for sure." Kira glanced at the galley. "I need some food."

"We just stocked up on everything, so you have your pick," Sven told her.

"Hmm." Kira wandered over to the cabinets and began perusing the selection. After checking in a couple places, she came across a packet of instant macaroni and cheese. She snatched it up. "Comfort food it is."

Sven eyed her from the table. "I take it the upgrades haven't been a smooth transition?"

<He knows,> Jasmine interjected.

<He might just be making conversation.> Kira began preparing the food packet with some hot water. "I've never had an AI before. It—"

"Kira, we've known each other for years. This ship isn't very big. We heard your team talking."

<Okay, so he does know.> Kira set the half-prepared macaroni on the countertop and turned around to face the systems engineer. "Yes, my modifications are a little more extensive than just a new AI."

"Is it really the nanites from the MTech lab?" Sven's brown eyes were wide with wonder.

"I can't get into the details, but suffice it to say there isn't anyone else quite like me."

He shook his head. "It's crazy to think about."

"You're tellin' me." With a sigh, Kira grabbed her bowl of cheesy pasta off the counter. It had finished hydrating and now looked indistinguishable from the fresh version her mom had made for her as a kid back home. *Gotta love modern science.*

"What else was MTech researching, you think?" Sven mused.

Kira sat down across from him. "I'd rather not know."

He placed his elbows on the tabletop and leaned forward. "Not even a little bit curious?"

"They had a handful of tech that was more advanced than it should be, given their overall capabilities. Questions about how they gained access to those developments lead down wormholes I'd rather not travel." Kira took a forkful of her meal and blew on it.

<Denial doesn't accomplish anything,> Jasmine said in her mind.

<I have enough problems to worry about right now without wondering what else these aliens in Gaelon may have been up to beyond genetics research.>

<We'll have to face that reality in a matter of hours,> the AI pointed out. *<I don't think they'll say, 'Oh, never mind' if we come across some of their technology that we don't like.>*

<Ha.>

Jasmine tsked. *<I'm serious. They seem to have access to extremely advanced science, even if they didn't invent any of it themselves.>*

The comment caught Kira by surprise. *<What makes you think the aliens didn't make these changes to the nanites?>*

<No, they're certainly behind that modification. But it's imperfect. For having a nanoscopic component of their own being—based on what's known about their 'remnants' on Valta—they don't have very good mastery of the form. That suggests to me that it's appropriated technology rather than something they've cultivated from the get-go.>

Thinking about the issues with how the nanites interfaced with her, Kira had wondered the same thing. Monica herself didn't seem to fully understand the technology, so her research could only take it so far. They had succeeded in making Kira a functional Robus, but she was far from perfect in that form.

True masters of the technology would have been able to adapt it by the time she came into the picture. MTech had had *years* to study subjects. That meant that the Trols had done the best they could, and it still wasn't good enough.

Kira didn't like the implications of that realization. *<If nanotech isn't their specialization, what is?>*

<Wouldn't we all like to know.>

<What could it be?>

Jasmine gave a mental shrug. *<Whatever it is, it was enough to give them a broad base of knowledge to semi-successfully adapt technology created by another, very different race. They're smart and resourceful, if nothing else.>*

<That makes the Trols sound like scavengers.>

<Maybe they are. But some of the most prolific lifeforms let others do the work for them.>

Kira frowned. *<I guess Tarans aren't all that different, are we? We've taken from others whenever it benefits us.>*

"You okay?" Sven asked.

"Yes, sorry," Kira returned to the world around her. "I suddenly understand that faraway look people with AIs sometimes get in the middle of a conversation."

Sven laughed. "Yeah, that can happen. Just don't forget to turn off any valves."

She raised a questioning eyebrow and continued eating her macaroni.

"This guy, Kevin, who I worked with some years back became friends with our ship's AI," the engineer explained. "The two of them used to get into arguments over the comms—probably two of the most stubborn individuals I've ever met. Sometimes, they'd go at it over their direct communication chip link instead. On this particular occasion, we were doing maintenance on some systems, which involved topping off the various gases."

Kira swallowed a particularly large mouthful. "Uh oh."

"Yeah, you can see where this is going." Sven smiled. "So, we're working away, and I looked over and notice that Kevin has that blank look he would get whenever talking with the AI. His face is beet red, so I can tell they're really in the heat of it. I go about my work, since I knew by then that I'd get an earful if I tried to interrupt their discussion.

"Several minutes go by, and by this point it's kinda like, 'Hash this out on your own time', ya know? So, I give Kevin one of those 'get-back-to-work' looks. When he doesn't react, I walk over to say it to his face. I get out 'Hey!' before I realize my voice is two octaves higher. Foking idiot opened the helium valve and never closed it!"

Kira laughed. "I bet that got his attention."

"Yeah, get this." A grin split Sven's face. "He yells 'Oh, shite!' in this chipmunk voice and shuts off the valve. The ship's AI comes over the comm to yell at him for being reckless, and Kevin replies, 'I can't have a dignified discussion like this!' That became my crew's favorite catchphrase—while doing an impression, of course."

"Wow." Kira thought for a moment. "Is it pretty easy to do something like that with helium?"

"Fairly. Why?" Sven tilted his head.

"Curious about what happens behind the scenes in these ships, that's all."

<Oh, no. What are you planning?> Jasmine asked in Kira's mind.

<Just getting ideas, nothing to worry about,> she assured her AI.

<This is about Ari, isn't it?>

<And if it is?>

<Then I like the way you think.> Jasmine gave her the mental equivalent of a smirk.

<Jasmine, I think we're going to get along just fine.> Kira returned her attention to Sven. "It's important to be able to make light of situations. We have stressful jobs, but we can't allow that to get the better of us."

Sven nodded. "Very true. That's why I have my writing."

"Creative outlets are a great way to stay sane."

"Well, writing can drive you a bit mad, sometimes," he countered. "I mean, we're literally writing down the conversations we have with voices in our heads."

Kira frowned. "That does sound a little off, when you put it that way."

"As long as we don't mutter too loudly to ourselves in public places, no one seems to mind."

"There is that." Kira glanced at the clock on the wall and saw that it was almost time for her team's workout. She grabbed her empty bowl and rose from the table. "Well, Sven, it's been great, but I need to get back to it."

He nodded and stood up across the table. "I should probably check in on everything, too." He paused. "And, if you ever do need access to some, uh, 'malfunctioning' helium tanks, let me know."

Kira grinned. "I'll do that."

— — —

Work in Leon's lab was starting to feel routine. While Tess and Jack were busy with their own tasks, Leon finished his review of the latest automated test results that had been kicked over to him for review.

To his relief, the scans didn't contain anything that

resembled the TRs they'd observed in others. "I'm glad there's nothing to worry about in these, but I wonder why the system is flagging so many?" he said to no one in particular.

Tess looked up from her desk across the lab. "Do you see any common factor between them?"

"Nothing that's jumping out at me," he replied. He'd been over the likely candidate criteria—age, aptitudes, genetic markers—but he was able to find an exception to each of the potential causes for the anomaly.

"Maybe it is just a genuine, random error, then," Tess said with a shrug.

"Perhaps." Leon didn't like that non-explanation, but he had nothing else to go on at the present.

With his task list of semi-critical items clear, Leon decided to run an updated sequence on Kira's nanites. The model would make a good baseline for how she was responding to the new pairing with Jasmine. He hoped her next check-in would show reduced stress levels, compared to where they'd been the past week. Maybe Jack would even be able to glean something about the nanites' transformation triggers, like Tess had suggested.

He took a blood sample from the suspension case they used for preservation and entered it into their commandeered sequencer for analysis. It was still unclear if MTech would demand the equipment be returned to them, but Leon suspected that no one who cared was still working at the company. A lot of people connected with MTech and the Mysaran government would be getting a fresh start, and with that staff turnover came the opportunity for convenient appropriations.

Their loss is the Guard's gain. After what he'd gone through in the lab—being misled, getting shot at, and having his girlfriend turned into a science experiment—he considered a few pieces of equipment to be a modest severance package.

Leon was just finishing up his configurations of the sequencer when an alert popped up on his desktop. It was a call from Mysar.

Either MTech is demanding their equipment back, or an old friend is reaching out, he figured.

While he didn't have too many friends left on Mysar, he'd spent enough time on the planet in grad school to establish lasting relationships. Any number of people may have heard by now that he'd been connected to the MTech lab on Valta, and a 'Hey, glad you didn't die!' message wouldn't be out of place.

He activated the sequencer and then directed the call to a private room across the hall, which was equipped for that very purpose. Large enough to hold two people, the room consisted of two chairs, a small table, and a viewscreen mounted to the wall.

Leon initiated the call as soon as he was inside. To his surprise, he saw his sister's face staring back at him. "Ellen? What are you doing on Mysar again?"

"Good to see you, too, Leon," she replied with a curl to her lips. "I'm here for business."

"Stars, not again..."

"*Official* business this time," she emphasized.

"And what does that entail?"

She smiled. "Helping put the pieces back together."

According to her recent track record, she's a whole lot better at making things fall apart. Leon decided it was best to keep that overly antagonistic comment to himself. "I hope it goes smoothly for you," he offered instead.

"It's off to a pretty good start."

Leon thought for a moment. "Say, since you're there,

would you check in on the testing they're doing for those telepathic receptors? Some people are getting flagged here, and we're not sure why. I'm clearing everyone on a case-by-case basis, but it would be much easier for someone to slip through the cracks in a civilian population."

"That's not really why I'm here, but I can mention it," Ellen said.

"Thanks." He looked her over. "So, was this just meant as a social call?"

"Not exclusively, but we didn't really get a chance to catch up before," Ellen replied. "How's Kira doing?"

A dull ache formed in Leon's chest hearing her name. This wasn't the time to be apart—and he especially didn't like her going to Gaelon. Playing into the enemy's hand sounded like a terrible idea. Maybe it was necessary, but they hadn't even taken the time to determine if there were alternatives.

"Uh, Leon?" his sister prompted.

"Sorry, it's been a long few days. She's okay. Adjusting."

Ellen nodded. "I just about shite myself when she transformed."

"Yeah, I know that feeling." His stomach flipped, remembering what it had been like to see Kira lose herself the first time.

"I can't believe someone was evil enough to do that to her," Ellen murmured.

Leon knew that his sister was under a similar NDA to the one he'd signed when joining the Guard, so she was likely looking for someone to talk to who was also in the inner circle. After what she'd witnessed with Kira's transformation and the Mysaran chancellor, the Tararian Guard had deemed it necessary to debrief her, including disclosure about elements of MTech's work. She had already figured out the alien possession related to Hale, so drawing a connection between the subversion and the bizarre experimentation wasn't a stretch.

"The capacity for evil never ceases to astound me," Leon agreed.

Ellen slumped. "I've met some of the people who were subverted here on Mysar. It's awful. They remember what they did, but it's like this half-recalled nightmare that keeps nagging at the back of their minds."

"I can't imagine being a prisoner within myself like that."

"What Kira did for Cynthia Hale…" Ellen swallowed. "It was a kindness, no matter what anyone may say otherwise."

"I heard about that." Leon looked down. "Kira hasn't wanted to talk about what happened on Mysar."

"I wouldn't have believed any of it if I hadn't seen it for myself. She transformed into that 'Robus state', and it's like she skipped across the room. I've never seen anything move so fast. And those teeth and claws… it was terrifying and awing at the same time."

"I've seen them. Definitely don't want to be on the receiving end."

"Better stay on her good side." Ellen cracked a smile.

"I knew better than to cross Kira even before that," Leon replied. Even as a teenager, Kira's 'I am not amused' glare had been legendarily dagger-like. He'd been the recipient exactly once, and from that point on, he'd chosen his words very carefully.

"How are things going with you two, by the way?" Ellen asked. "You being an item kind of came out of nowhere."

"Not really. We were together for a long time."

"Yeah, a *decade* ago. Had you stayed in touch?"

"No, hadn't seen her or communicated a word since we

broke up."

She tilted her head and raised an eyebrow in the judging-older-sister pose he'd always detested. "So why now?"

"Because we reconnected, and there was still something there. I don't think I need to explain myself."

"It's just surprising, that's all."

It was Leon's turn to give her a nonplussed look. "And why is that?"

"You always seemed so committed to your work."

Yeah, to fill a void. Leon hadn't realized until he'd reconnected with Kira that he'd initially thrown himself into his work as a way to deal with their sudden breakup. One day they had been talking about moving to Mysar together for school, and the next, Kira said she was joining the Guard. He'd never learned why she'd changed her mind, though he'd been trying to find the right time to ask her. School and work had been his escape from that unresolved relationship, and by the time he was emotionally healed, focusing on his career was a way of life.

"My work is still important to me," Leon replied to his sister. "But there's room for other things, too."

"You uprooted your entire existence to follow her to the Guard."

"Ellen, you do realize that I'm now working with an organization that has galactic reach, right? Kira or not, this was a great job opportunity."

"But what about Valta?"

Leon crossed his arms. "Is this coming from Mom and Dad?"

"Oh, don't get me started on them." She sighed. "I've only talked to them once since everything went down with MTech, and that entire conversation was about how we'd both abandoned them."

"Seriously?"

She shrugged. "I learned years ago not to let it get to me. You have to follow your own path."

"Well, I didn't have a lot of prospects left on Valta, with the MTech lab getting condemned and all."

"You don't think they'll reopen?"

"Ellen, I honestly have no clue what kind of future MTech will have. Their leadership was being controlled by telepathic aliens. I don't know if there is anybody willing to pick up the torch and rebuild the company into something worthy of contributing to the Taran Empire. That's your area, not mine."

She evaluated him over the screen. "You said that like Mysar was part of the Empire."

"If you're there, I assume that's the plan for the world. With Elusia rejoined, I can only imagine Mysar and Valta aren't far behind."

"That's my hope, yes," Ellen admitted. "It'll take some convincing."

"Do you think you'll be successful?"

"It's not a matter of that. I think it's *inevitable*. This universe is too vast, and the challenges are too great, for us to consider facing it alone."

Leon's eyes widened. "Wow, you've come around since your Sovereign days."

"I've seen another, better way. People are allowed to change."

"It's encouraged."

"And I'm a better person for it." She looked down and took a slow breath. "I didn't mean to judge your relationship with Kira. I just don't want you to get hurt."

"What makes you think I would?"

She hesitated. "As committed as you were to your work, Kira is in the Guard. That's a lifestyle, not just a job."

"I know, and I accept that."

"But do you *really*? It doesn't bother you when she goes off on a mission to stars-know-where and is getting shot at or being infected with experimental nanites?"

Leon's eyes narrowed. "What kind of question is that? *Of course* it bothers me. But I accept it as a reality, and I'd never ask her to change who she is for me."

Ellen smiled and chuckled to herself.

"What?" Leon demanded, a bite in his voice.

"You passed the test."

"Huh?"

Ellen met his gaze, soft and compassionate. "You love and accept her for who she is. Too many people fall in love with someone and expect them to be molded into the partner they want to have. But you understand what you're getting into. That's real. That's what lasts."

Leon relaxed. "Oh, that."

"I know, sage analysis from the person who hasn't ever held down a relationship for more than six months. But still, I know something that'll last when I see it. I just haven't been lucky enough to find that for myself."

"I'm in this one for the long haul, so you better say something now if you have concerns," Leon cautioned.

"I hope the Guard has dental insurance, because those fangs—"

"Ellen!"

She laughed. "Sorry, I couldn't resist." His sister composed herself. "But seriously, I'm really happy you two got back together. I always liked her for you."

"Thanks, me too."

Ellen straightened. "Oh! So I said this was partially a social call, but I did have one official bit of news to pass along."

"What's that?" Leon asked.

"I have a feeling something still isn't right on Mysar."

Leon wiped his hands down his face. "Ellen, not again. I won't be your intermediary for getting help from the Guard."

She bristled. "I'm not requesting help. I'm just letting you know that I'm not yet convinced the problem was completely taken care of when Hale and her possessor died."

"Well—" Leon bit his tongue.

"What were you about to say?"

"Um." Leon wished he were better at backpedaling. "Just because Hale died, that doesn't mean the alien presence died, too. It's possible that only its control point was severed."

"That thing could still be alive?"

"Possibly. I can't be certain," he hedged, "but we'll have more information once Kira and her team get back from their current mission."

"Shite! How many more of those things are out there?"

"I have no idea. We think they're based in Gaelon," he revealed.

Ellen slumped back in her chair, dropping her image to the bottom half of the screen. "They were our neighbors this whole time?"

"Keep that need-to-know," he cautioned. "I probably shouldn't have said anything to *you*, but since you're investigating what went on there—what might still be going on—it seems like good information to have in the back of your mind."

She nodded absently. "Yes, thanks. I'll learn what I can."

"Be careful, Ellen. We don't know the extent of what these aliens can do."

"Don't worry about me. I can't possibly get myself into as much trouble as I did last time."

Leon sucked in a breath. "Please don't take that as a personal challenge."

She laughed. "No. I'm over trying to fix everything myself. My recent glimpse behind the scenes at how the Guard operates was a good reminder of how it's best to let an experienced team of pros handle the heavy lifting."

"All right, I'll hold you to it."

"Won't be a problem."

Leon nodded. "Okay. Well, let us know if you come across anything concrete. I suspect we'll learn a lot more on this end over the next day or two."

"Good luck," Ellen wished him back. "If there's something still amiss, we'll find out what it is and fix it."

CHAPTER 6

THE *RAVEN* DROPPED out of subspace at the navigation beacon that serviced the Elvar Trinary. Rather than its previous route into that system, the ship instead veered toward the adjacent Gaelon System—the place Kira had always been taught to avoid.

In retrospect, she should have questioned the travel ban. Rarely were places completely off-limits. Of course, some systems had more environmental hazards than were worth messing with, but the fact that no one had ever given a definitive reason as to *why* Gaelon was such a bad place should have raised suspicions.

As the *Raven* glided into Gaelon space in stealth mode, a feeling of profound disquiet overtook Kira. She wandered into the galley and stood by the back viewport, which afforded a clear survey of the starscape beyond. It appeared peaceful… but anything could be lurking in the black.

What kind of countermeasures do they have in place? If no one has documented the details of this system before, there has to be something keeping people from reporting back.

<Kira, what are you thinking about? Your heart rate just spiked.>

<Sorry, Jasmine,> Kira replied. <I was wondering how the Trols managed to keep people out of this system for so long. I grew up with stories that it was dangerous, but is that mythos enough?>

<It's more than folklore. There have been eight known disappearances in the system,> Jasmine stated. <People typically don't like to go places where there's a risk they may never be seen again.>

<Only eight? I'd think more people would have tried to investigate it by now.>

<There may be more that were never officially recorded. After all, travelers going after that kind of location might not exactly be operating within the law.>

<Like smugglers,> Kira realized. <That kind of system would appeal to those sorts.>

<Precisely. I can't say if any have tried to venture inside, but it wouldn't surprise me.>

<It fits the narrative, that's for sure.> Kira crossed her arms. The chill of space seemed to suddenly seep through the viewport.

<Even accounting for smugglers and the like, the scale of visitors would only be in the dozens, or maybe hundreds,> Jasmine continued. <Dispensing with so few ships would be easy for a race as advanced as the Trols.>

<You say that like it's normal to hide an entire civilization in a star system.>

<Don't forget the vastness of space, Kira. It's really a wonder the Empire hasn't run into more sentient life already.>

Kira sighed. <You're always too logical.>

<It's that bomaxed computer part of me. Can't quite get away from it.> Jasmine winked in her mind.

<Yet, somehow you understand sarcasm.>

<I am multifaceted. It's what makes me unique.>

Kira softened. *<I'm glad you're here with me, Jasmine. I was nervous about getting paired with an AI, but it means a lot to have someone to talk to right now. I don't feel like I can be completely open with my team about everything I'm going through.>*

<Colonel Kaen and Major Sandren are wise. I don't think they would have nudged you in this direction if they didn't think you could benefit from the arrangement.>

<They had their own motivations. They wanted my skills to figure out what's going on with the Trols.>

Jasmine tsked. *<Kira, you want answers as much as the rest of the Guard—maybe more. Don't pretend like you didn't want to go on this op.>*

<Ugh, it's like you're in my head or something.>

<Better get used to it!>

Kira stared out the viewport for another three minutes before she decided to go down one deck to the recreation level, where most members of the crew were congregated.

As she hopped off the ladder, Kira spotted the three soldiers on her team, along with Sven, and Gil—the *Raven*'s mechanic—lounging on the couches around the main screen in the rec room. Some mindless comedy movie was playing, but Kira didn't recognize it.

The group erupted into laughter at a joke that must have been referencing something earlier in the film.

Nia happened to look over and notice Kira watching them. "Join us!" she called out.

Kira moseyed over, stopping behind Sven where he was

seated on the couch. "I didn't realize there was a party going on down here."

Sven tilted his head back so he could see her. "You hurried off from our chat earlier before I got the chance to tell you."

"Oh, you two had a heart-to-heart?" Ari raised an eyebrow.

"I demoed all my best dance moves for him," Kira shot back.

"She did, and it was glorious," Sven said, playing along.

She patted the engineer's shoulder. "Good bonding time. The rest of you shouldn't have been so quick to nap."

Kyle pursed his lips. "Aren't you the one who told us to always rest when we get the chance because we never know what's ahead?"

Kira smiled. "Do as I say, not as I do."

"Great leadership, Kira," Nia ribbed.

"It's a gift."

"Approaching Gaelon System heliopause," said a female voice Kira recognized as belonging to Aleya, the *Raven*'s first officer.

"Social hour is over," Kira announced.

"Work, work, work." Kyle rose from the couch, followed by the others as they let out weary sighs.

"Don't sound so enthused, everyone." Kira's gaze passed over the team. They looked far more worn and tired than usual.

She felt it, too. They'd been on the go for almost two weeks straight, which was significantly more intensive than their usual routine. Add in the disproportionate number of firefights, and they'd experienced at least two months' worth of action in that short span.

Kira wished she could offer them some relief, but there was no one else. They were the best team for the job; beyond that, she trusted them. There simply wasn't anyone else with whom she'd walk into such an unknown, dangerous situation.

"We'll rest easy when we know the bad guys are no longer a threat," Nia said on behalf of the group.

"You and me both," Kira agreed. "I'll go see what we're working with and report back in the galley."

Being such a small ship, there wasn't a designated briefing area on the vessel. The galley served double duty as a meal space, card table, and a gathering place to discuss mission details.

Before they could have an effective conversation, however, Kira needed to learn what they were up against. She scaled the ladder to the operations deck, where Major Sandren was waiting outside the bridge.

"Get any rest?" he asked her.

"A little. Jasmine and I have been bonding."

"Best of buddies now," Jasmine said over the audible comms.

Sandren smiled. "Glad to hear it. Let's go talk with Aleya and Rodrick to see if they can tell us any more about this system."

"Sounds like a plan, sir."

Sandren stepped forward and knocked on the door.

The hatch popped open.

"Come in," a male voice stated.

Kira hadn't interacted with Rodrick, the *Raven*'s captain, on many occasions, but the quiet ex-fighter pilot had always struck her as a measured force to have in command. Whatever observations he and Aleya might make during the upcoming discussion, Kira vowed to listen.

The bridge of the ship was surprisingly spacious, compared to the other accommodations. It consisted of two control panels in the front, accompanied by ergonomic chairs, a central holodisplay used for course plotting and displaying scan results, and two workstations along the side walls, which offered space for additional crew members to directly interface with the ship's advanced sensor suite.

"What kind of backwater hole did you bring us to this time, sir?" Rodrick asked Sandren from the captain's seat.

The major chuckled. "We thought getting a reminder about our place in the universe might do everyone some good."

Kira didn't know the details, but she'd heard that Rodrick had trained under Sandren when he had first joined the Guard. They'd maintained a good-natured rapport over the years, and she'd often observed their interactions to be more casual than most conducted with the major. Then again, her own relationship with Sandren was on the casual side, so maybe that was just how he was. Sometimes a personal connection trumped rank when it came to face-to-face, but everyone knew the chain of command when they were in the thick of it.

Sandren stood in the center of the bridge with his hands clasped, and Kira took up a position next to him.

"We're processing the initial readings now," Aleya reported. "As long-range scans had indicated, there's some strange radiation in the system. We haven't identified a source yet, but these first readings may help narrow it down."

Kira watched the data populate on the central holodisplay. It was by no means her specialization, but something about the readings looked strange.

"Does this seem unusual to anyone?" she asked to no one in particular, pointing to a dark patch on the visual representation of the system. The map included an overlay of the radiation, electromagnetic, and other relevant properties in each area.

"I was thinking the same thing," Aleya agreed.

"The readings make it look like there's a dwarf planet there, but the gravitational models indicate that there shouldn't be anything there," observed Rodrick.

Kira frowned. "So, mystery planet?"

"Or something else." Rodrick sighed. "We'll need to get close enough to get visual confirmation."

"Only problem with that is getting close to something that may be dangerous," Sandren cautioned.

"Isn't that what we came here to do, sir?" Kira questioned. "We crossed over that danger threshold when we decided to come here in the first place."

"Our stealth tech is solid," Rodrick added. "There are no guarantees they can't detect us, but we're certainly not waving a flashing sign saying that we're here. It's possible we can get closer for an inspection without being spotted."

"Then we have to try," Sandren said. "What else are we working with in the system? Any other anomalies?"

"Nothing else that distinctive," Aleya replied, "though there is a gas giant on the other side of the system." She frowned.

"What is it?" Sandren prompted.

"It may be nothing." The first officer crossed her arms. "The odd, dark spot that may be a dwarf planet and this gas giant are exactly opposite the star from each other right now."

"So?" Kira asked.

She nodded. "It's probably coincidence, but given the weird readings, it seemed worth noting."

Sandren stroked his chin. "We'll keep it in mind."

<This isn't the kind of symmetry found in nature,> Jasmine commented to Kira.

<I was wondering about that. Bets on what we'll find?>

<Evil alien secret moon base,> the AI replied.

Kira scowled. *<Are you being serious?>*

<There's a fine line between fact and facetiousness.>

<I'm not sure there actually is...> Kira ventured.

<When you need to find a way to amuse yourself for hours while you travel at sub-light, sometimes you need to get creative with your non-fiction. We still have another twelve hours to go.>

<Ugh.> Kira sighed.

<Blame physics.>

Kira chuckled in her mind. *<That doesn't sound very scientist-like.>*

<After you've done enough science, you get cynical. Do you have any idea how many microprocesses I can complete in twelve hours? I'll tune back in when we're there.>

<What will you be working on?>

<Trying to figure out what's going on with you, of course,> Jasmine replied. *<You're quite the specimen, Kira.>*

<Now that sounded like a scientist. And ultra-creepy.>

<I promise to dissect you gently.>

<How very reassuring.>

Sandren was still studying the system map on the holodisplay. "Are you able to overlay the data we gathered when the control signal was traced from Jared to the system?"

Aleya nodded. "Yes. Not surprisingly, it traced back to the strange, dark area."

"I'm going to venture that's *not* a coincidence," Kira chimed in.

"Certainly not." Sandren agreed. "The question is, what's capable of creating that kind of distortion?"

"It might be some kind of stealth technology," Rodrick suggested. "We couldn't detect anything anomalous from a distance, and what's more, we can't determine the nature of the body—just that there's something strange going on there."

"That would be more than enough cloaking if they're able to keep people out of the system," Kira assessed.

Sandren tapped his index finger beneath his lower lip. "Very true. And what about the radiation?"

"It's a relatively low level, but it's almost everywhere," Aleya replied. "Nothing our shields can't handle, but it's a high enough concentration that some civilian vessels might have trouble, if they hung around for too long."

"A deterrent?" Kira asked.

"Irradiating an entire system is a tall order," Sandren replied.

"But not unfeasible."

"True," the major conceded, "and these Gaelons have demonstrated that they're willing to go to great lengths."

"We're going to make a push to call them 'Trols'," Kira interjected.

Sandren thought about it for a second. "That does sound way better."

Kira smiled. "Sometimes it's all about the branding."

CHAPTER 7

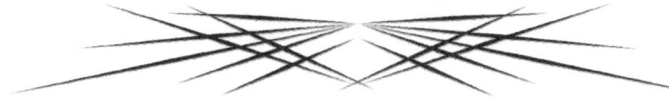

THE SITUATION ON Mysar was more concerning than Ellen had anticipated. She raised her gaze from the personnel records displayed on the table in front of her.

"This isn't why I came here," she stated to Trisha. "We would have sent someone else—or a whole team—to help, had we known."

The other woman wrung her hands. "I know, but we weren't sure if we could trust Elusia. If we requested you—"

Ellen groaned. "I'm no one special."

"You've lived on Mysar! Most Elusians either hate this world or are indifferent, at best."

"Trisha, you have a serious issue with government stability right now. I can't fix this alone."

As Ellen had dug into the present state of affairs, she'd made an alarming discovery. While a number of the government officials were still physically present, many had never been in full control of their actions for the duration of their tenure. Far more people than she'd been led to believe. When Leon had asked her to look into the testing, she never dreamed that almost *everyone* who'd been working for the government would be flagged as a potential risk.

Aside from that concern, there was the political component. When she volunteered for the assignment, her assumption had been that there were frontrunner candidates already lined up to take over as chancellor. Now she wasn't sure anyone wanted the job.

They want me to make recommendations for new leaders, but how many of these people truly know how to do their jobs— or even want this as a career? She wasn't sure how to proceed.

"We didn't mean to mislead you," Trisha continued. "If there are people you can trust, bring them in."

"You're missing my point. *I* shouldn't be the person leading this effort in the first place. And how can you possibly trust *me* when I've switched allegiance?"

"Because you changed your views in the interest of bringing our people together." Trisha looked her in the eyes. "That's the mindset we need right now."

"But still." Ellen massaged the bridge of her nose. "All right, look, we need to gather a better baseline for what people remember while Reya was in control."

Trisha's eyebrows drew together. "Reya?"

"That was the name of the presence controlling Chancellor Hale," Ellen explained.

The other woman's face drained. "I didn't know it had a name."

"That's how it identified itself, anyway. We've only encountered one other being like it. That one could only control one person at a time, except for short bursts in which it could influence others to perform a specific task."

"But Reya was…?"

"That's what we need to find out," Ellen continued. "We

know it was using Hale as a hub, but what was the nature of the control over the others? I have a list of three dozen people here who held the most senior positions in the Mysaran government, and all admitted to having at least one memory gap that suggests they were subverted by Reya. Did they ever actually do their jobs, and do them well? Or did their political prowess come from Reya's influence? I can't begin to make recommendations about anyone's fitness to lead until I know more about what was done to them."

"What do you need? How can I help?" Trisha's eager tone had a hint of desperation that concerned Ellen, but she'd take that enthusiasm over indifference.

"I guess we need to have interviews with some people and see what insights they can share," Ellen responded. *And, hopefully, someone will express interest in their job.*

"Do you have anyone in mind, or should I make some selections?"

Ellen looked over the personnel list again. "Bring in Garett Steckler and Fiona Wyles, then select three others at random."

Trisha nodded. "One at a time or in a group?"

"Individually," Ellen instructed. "I'll wait here."

"I'll send Fiona in first," Trisha acknowledged and departed to summon the requested people.

Ellen rose from the table and turned around to gaze out the window at the city below. People were still going about their lives like nothing had changed. *Would they be so calm if they realized no one was really running this world right now?*

She knew she'd be freaking out. If she weren't in the inner circle regarding the matter, she'd consider cutting her losses and moving somewhere with less drama, where she could live out a peaceful life. But, people were counting on her. Not to mention she was beginning to suspect she was addicted to drama.

Five minutes later, a knock sounded on the door. A petite woman with dark complexion entered.

Ellen recognized her from the photo in her personnel file. "Hi, Fiona, my name is Ellen Calleti. I've come from Elusia to offer my support while you rebuild the Mysaran government."

"Yes, I've heard about you," Fiona replied. She closed the door behind her.

"Word travels quickly," Ellen said with a smile.

"There's been a lot to talk about." Fiona slowly walked to the table and placed her hands on the back of a chair. "What's the particular matter you wanted to discuss with me?"

Ellen mirrored Fiona's stance on the opposite side of the table. "I wanted to learn more about your past work experience and your aspirations going forward."

Fiona raised an eyebrow. "To see if I'm qualified to do my job?"

"I'm not here to pass judgment on qualifications. But I do want to make sure people land where they want to be."

"That's an interesting distinction," Fiona said, tracing the seam in the fabric along the top of the chair with her index finger. "I always considered qualifications to be the most important factor when selecting someone for a job."

"Skills and experience don't carry the same weight when the person isn't committed to their position."

"I'll give you that." Fiona evaluated her. "Let's just cut to the heart of the issue. You want to know if I'm interested in being chancellor?"

She's certainly sharp, but I'm not getting the warm fuzzies from her. This might not be the kind of person we need right now.

Ellen flashed a curt smile. "That isn't the reason for this meeting. I only wanted to discuss your time working with Cynthia Hale."

"Ah." Understanding passed across Fiona's face. "Was I myself or was I subverted?"

"That's the ultimate question, yes." Ellen gestured to the chairs for them to sit.

Fiona pulled back the chair she had been standing behind and lowered herself with the grace of a dancer—or at least of someone who knew how to put on a good show. "Self-report doesn't make for an ideal evaluation tool."

"It doesn't," Ellen agreed, "but that's all we have. I hope that people are willing to be honest, for the sake of creating a good future on Mysar."

"You won't find any opposition from me. To that end, I'll tell you that I shouldn't be chancellor."

Didn't see that coming. Given the woman's previous statements, Ellen had been certain Fiona was interested. "Why not?" Ellen asked.

"For the very reason you're using nonverbal tactics to equalize the power balance between us, consciously or not. I have enough self-awareness to recognize that I'm not the kind of person who sets others at ease. You're on the defensive. I'm an acquired taste, and that's not the right person to have as the face of a planet."

Ellen chuckled. "I'd argue that level of understanding is *precisely* what would make you a good leader."

Fiona shrugged. "Perhaps. But to your point earlier, I don't want the job." She smiled. "Besides, you said that's not why we're meeting."

"Right." Ellen refocused on the task at hand. "Your time with Chancellor Hale."

"I was something like an enforcer for her," Fiona continued. "She liked my brand of bite. Now, to answer the question you keep talking around: I was me, to the best of my recollection. I'm certain she influenced me now and then, but I can trace the logic of my actions back to my own thoughts and feelings. I was convinced I was doing good work."

"And what was the work you did as an enforcer?" Ellen prompted.

"When others needed help with being convinced to do their own assigned tasks, I would pay them a visit. I think Hale liked to send me because I don't look intimidating, and I could catch people off-guard when I went to put them in their place."

"Is there any particular matter where people needed extra convincing?"

Fiona's show of composed strength cracked the slightest measure. "Yes, there was something. A facility that we weren't supposed to talk about."

Ellen came to attention. "What was it?"

"I don't know what they did in there, but it was more common than not for people to spend one day there and not want to go back. I'd need to convince them that it would be a mistake to abandon their post."

"Did anyone ever say *why* they didn't want to go back?"

Fiona shook her head. "I never went there myself—Hale made sure I didn't. But the workers would talk about The Pit and how they didn't like how it got inside their heads. I thought they were crazy at the time."

A chill washed over Ellen. "Where is this facility located?"

"Outside of town, midway between the capitol building and the city. It doesn't look like much from the outside, but I hear there's an underground superstructure."

"How did you convince people to work there?" Ellen asked

tentatively.

Fiona crossed her arms. "I used Hale's words, not mine. The meaning is pretty different, now that I know what was really going on. I was told to tell them that if they didn't go there of their own accord, they would be 'compelled to comply'."

"And they listened to that?"

The other woman shook her head slowly. "Not always. I mean, I was good at my job, and it's a small enough place that people typically needed to follow the work. But when they didn't listen... when I saw them again, they were different. *That* was what true subversion looks like."

"Has anyone been to that facility since Hale's death?"

"No."

Ellen fixed Fiona in a level gaze. "I know I don't need to spell out the reason for you. Will you go there with me?"

Fiona nodded. "I wouldn't have mentioned it otherwise."

Ellen activated the comm controls via the tabletop. "Trisha, cancel those other meetings. We're going to take a field trip."

CHAPTER 8

IT WAS THE times when missions took Kira to places away from navigation beacon network when she was reminded that space was really big. And empty.

Kira paced in front of the galley viewport while she waited to catch their first sight of what had appeared to be a dark spot on the system scans. She was one hundred percent certain they'd find something there, but it was anyone's guess what it might be.

<*It'll be that world you saw in your vision,*> Jasmine supplied.

<*You sound awfully sure about that.*>

<*That's where the logic takes me.*>

<*It's illogical that nanoscopic aliens that band together as interstellar telepathic entities would live on a planet resembling a pastoral painting.*>

<*Why?*> Jasmine asked in a matter-of-fact mental tone.

<*Because it is?*> Kira replied, not sure how to assign logic to that instinct.

<*We know these beings spent time on Valta,*> Jasmine

continued, *<and that's a quintessential landscape, as you'd describe it. Perhaps there is something in these beings' history that draws them to such locations. Or, it may be grounded in the science underlying those places, such as the oxygen and carbon ratios, or a similar factor. Either way, you glimpsed something that had significance to Reya. I wouldn't dismiss it.>*

Kira sighed. *<Okay, fine, so pastoral planet it is. How do we go about exploring a place like that?>*

<That's your expertise, not mine. I'm just here to keep you from going all Robus-y on your team.>

<Really, Jasmine, that's how you're going to play this?>

The AI laughed. *<Kira, I'm here whenever you need me. But you've seen inside the minds of these beings, I haven't. Trust your instincts.>*

"Am I interrupting?" a familiar voice said from the galley entrance.

Kira turned to see Kyle entering. "No, just chatting with Jasmine," she replied. "We're anxious to see what we're facing."

"Nia and Ari are taking bets. My money is on a space station."

"Jasmine thinks it'll be the planet I saw," Kira told him.

"That's what Nia thought, too. We're coming up on the twelve-hour mark, right? Should know any minute."

Kira looked back out the viewport. "I'm already trying to plan out how we can possibly investigate something that large."

"Big things always have smaller parts that are decidedly more interesting. We'll go after those."

"I'm used to opponents that operate like us," Kira mused. "Individuals, society, computer networks, transportation systems. These Trols defy all that."

"But *you* can interface with them." Kyle came to stand next to her. "We have every confidence in you, Kira."

<As do I,> Jasmine interjected in Kira's mind.

I guess I'd better deliver—

Kira's private thoughts were interrupted by a glimpse of a new point of light in the starscape out the viewport. She magnified it using the holographic overlay on the viewport.

"That's a planet!" she exclaimed.

Kyle peered into the darkness. "Fok, it is." He groaned. "Now I'll have to pay up to Nia."

"What did you wager this time?"

"Just his dignity," Nia said from the galley entry.

Kira and Kyle turned around.

Nia held out her arm, palm upturned, and curled her fingers in a beckoning fashion. "Come on, let's have it."

Kyle sighed and dropped to his knees. He gazed up at Nia as she leered over him. Kyle cleared his throat. "Nia is the wisest guesser there ever was, and her name shall echo throughout history as the greatest predictor ever known."

She looked at him expectantly.

"And she was right about this," Kyle added in a decidedly quieter and less enthused tone. He rolled his eyes.

Kira watched the exchange with crossed arms and a raised eyebrow. "Really, guys?"

"Well, money is irrelevant, and I don't need a genuine favor at the moment," Nia explained. "But, I mean, come on— I'll be able to lord this over him for weeks."

"I have no doubt we'll be hearing about it for some time." Kira shook her head. "If you're finished with the theatrics, I need to talk with the captain about this new planet."

She left Nia smirking at Kyle as he tried to explain the rationale behind his original prediction.

<Is that what passes for entertainment on your team?> Jasmine asked while Kira scaled the ladder.

<To Nia, yes. Ari prefers his blackmail videos. Pretty sure Kyle gets his kicks from psychoanalyzing people's computer password choices.>

Jasmine took a moment to respond. *<I was ready to call Kyle the weird one, but now I think he may be the most normal of all of you.>*

<You would think that.>

At the top of the access shaft, Kira headed toward the bridge's door. It was cracked open, and she entered.

Sandren was examining the holodisplay at the center of the room with Rodrick while Aleya piloted the craft.

"It's a planet," the major announced.

"So we've seen," Kira replied, stepping forward to stand across the holodisplay from him.

"But it's not *really* a planet," Rodrick clarified.

Kira's eyes narrowed. "What do you mean?"

"Well," Rodrick continued, "first of all, it would be a *dwarf* planet. But really, these scans are all wrong for a natural object. It's not nearly dense enough, and the materials are... strange."

"Can you quantify that?" Kira asked.

"Uh, lots of weird?" he said.

"That would have to be 'Weird Factor 7' to be properly quantified," Aleya chimed in from the controls.

"Right, that." Rodrick frowned at the holodisplay. "Basically, we've never seen anything like this, and the databanks aren't helpful."

Kira took a slow breath. "Okay, so we're dealing with a non-natural object the size of a dwarf planet. What about its other properties?"

"Well, it *looks* like a normal planet," Sandren replied. "Forests, mountains, oceans. However, it's lacking the usual markers for organic compounds."

"Not all life is carbon-based," Kira pointed out.

"Very true, but the arrangement of the structures on this planet is… designed." Rodrick zoomed in on a section of the world using the panel. "Like here, it's all perfectly mapped out. This isn't something that nature did on its own."

Kira had to admit there was something unnerving about the perfectly straight lines and divisions between different geographic elements. "Okay, so there's an artificial dwarf planet with manufactured environmental features. What else?"

"It's emitting a frequency we can't explain," Sandren stated.

"Let me guess: the same frequency we observed while tracing the signal from Jared back at base?" Kira asked.

"The very one," he confirmed. "Strong pulses with an underlying constant background hum."

"I guess we found the transmitter." She looked over the map. "Where's the origin point?"

"It seems to be everywhere," Rodrick told her. "We're still trying to sort through the data to get a more accurate reading. It has to be coming from *somewhere*, even if that's just the power source feeding into bio-speakers around the whole planet."

Kira nodded. "If you can identify the location, then that's where we need to go."

"This is a recon mission," Sandren countered.

"And the data we're gathering up here is being classified as 'weird' and 'strange', sir. If we're going to learn what's really going on with this structure, we need to get down there and gather samples or try to interface with it—something." Kira looked down. "And yes, I know it's entirely possible that this is a trap. I know they want me. But right now, finding out everything that we can is what's most important. The Guard and the safety of Empire's citizens come first."

Sandren inclined his head. "If the environmental conditions are reasonable, you're right. We do need some boots on the ground."

"Conditions are conducive to supporting life," Aleya confirmed. "Gravity is a little light, but way more than it should be, given the mass of this thing. There must be some sort of active artificial gravity."

"I'd suggest powered armor," Kira said. "Air recirc sounds a lot better than whatever particulates might be floating around down there."

"Agreed," Sandren confirmed. "Prep your team. We'll arrange a shuttle transport as soon as we have a target."

— — —

As if there weren't already enough red flags, Ellen had become convinced that the secret Mysaran facility was definitely trouble once she learned that the transit system didn't service the location. Though it was positioned almost in line with the city and the capitol building, it was at the base of a bizarre valley, which meant it was only accessible by shuttle.

True to Fiona's statement, the facility didn't look like more than a small house on the surface. Ellen would have missed it if she wasn't looking for a structure in that specific location. It was surrounded by rock formations unlike anything she'd seen elsewhere on the world—almost like dark waves arching from the red soil. The steep cliffs ringing the valley rose one hundred meters, making the place appear even more isolated.

"What were they doing out here?" she muttered to herself while staring out the shuttle viewport as they approached the landing site.

Trisha was seated in the row in front of her, and Fiona was across the aisle. The two other women had their eyes glued to the viewports next to their seats, as well.

"It has to be connected," Fiona replied.

"What do you mean?" Trisha asked.

Fiona didn't take her gaze off the viewport. "There's no way this place was only serviced by shuttle. There has to be another way in."

Ellen was inclined to agree, but she didn't like the implications. An out-of-the-way facility was one thing, but kilometers of underground tunnels took the conspiracy to a whole other level. Still, it was the most likely scenario, and she couldn't ignore evidence just because she didn't like what it indicated.

She knew from experience that there were multiple sublevels to the main government building. It was possible one of those contained a tunnel that spanned the six kilometers to the valley. *But why would they do that?*

So many other secrets had been kept in plain sight that it was odd that they'd have gone to the trouble of creating underground tunnels when a road or rail line would have increased the connection.

Because they didn't want others to know that the facility was there, let alone that it was connected to the government, she answered her own question. *Whatever is in there can't be good.*

The shuttle descended into a clearing between the wave-like rocks, and the side hatch opened. A wave of heat swept through the cabin.

Trisha scowled. "I hope they have air conditioning in this place."

"It's underground. We won't need it," Ellen replied. She rose from her seat and smoothed her pencil dress, which was paired with lightweight leggings and flat boots that were her most practical footwear for walking.

The three women walked down the ramp from the shuttle.

Dry air burned Ellen's lungs as she took a deep breath. She coughed. "Let's get inside."

Hewn of dark stone similar to the material of the rock waves, the facility's exterior façade rose one story and had a roof that angled down from a massive boulder next to it. There appeared to be no openings in the walls, aside from a single door.

Ellen picked up her pace to reach the door first. A control panel was enclosed inside a hinged protective cover next to the door, complete with a biometric scanner. She placed her hand on the device.

The screen flashed red, accompanied by 'Access Denied'.

"Let me try," Fiona offered, and Ellen moved out of her way.

When Fiona placed her hand on the screen, it changed to blue. The adjacent door hissed open.

"Good to know you're in their system," Ellen said to her.

"Not sure that's a system I *want* to be in."

Behind them, Trisha took a shaky breath. "I don't like this place."

Ellen stepped inside. "That makes all of us."

The five-by-five meter room looked more like an MTech lab than something found inside a stone shack at the bottom of a remote valley. Primarily finished in white, and well lit, the room was everything Ellen would envision for a sophisticated control room. Monitors lined the walls at three distinct workstations, and a sealed door was set into the wall that butted up to the boulder Ellen had observed from the outside.

"This is really weird," she said.

"I've heard others describe it, but this isn't what I imagined." Fiona looked around the room. "We need to get through that door."

Trisha held up her hand. "First, we need to gather any data we can from these computers."

"Agreed, there may be records here that we can't access elsewhere," Ellen said. "Fiona, you might need to do the honors, since you seem to be recognized in the system."

"I'll try." She stepped over to the closest workstation.

"Trisha, let's take a look at this door." Ellen walked over to it.

There was no handle, which indicated the door either swung inward or was controlled exclusively through an electronic panel. A shove against it confirmed that they wouldn't be able to open it manually.

"Where would you put controls?" Ellen scanned the vicinity until she spotted a scanner at waist level to the left side of the door. She extended her hand toward it.

"Wait!" Fiona called out.

Ellen paused. "Find something?"

"Yes. Shite, this is bad. We need to get out of here." Fiona raced toward the exit door.

"What is it?" Ellen stepped back from the side door, but she'd need more than vague statements to make her abandon their research expedition before it'd begun.

Fiona held up a portable data drive. "I downloaded the summary data. I think Reya is still here."

CHAPTER 9

ELLEN RAN WITH Fiona and Trisha to the waiting shuttle. "What makes you think Reya is here?" she asked.

"The login records," she explained while they climbed inside the craft. "Not just for the network, but for the facility here. There's a prefix code from each government office. I know the codes for the office in the city and the main capitol building near here, but I just saw a third prefix code which must be for this place. I noticed that the chancellor's old login access stopped when it should have, at the time of her death, but that account has been active from this facility within the past two days."

"Oh, shite," Trisha whispered.

Ellen swallowed. "And if I was a power-hungry alien megalomaniac like Reya, I'd be pissed that my plans were upset and looking to either reclaim what was lost or get revenge."

"Hence the 'let's get the fok out now' stance," Fiona said, accompanied by a hand flourish.

"Which now makes complete sense," Ellen acknowledged. *I'd really hoped Leon was wrong.*

"Great, so these beings don't die in the sense we're used to." Fiona shook her head.

Ellen looked over at the terrified faces of the two women. She needed to offer reassurance that they would get assistance in the upcoming fight.

"Right now, the Guard is investigating the place that they think is the aliens' home," Ellen revealed.

"They do exist in a specific place, then?" Hope returned to Fiona's eyes.

"We'll know soon." Ellen looked at the data drive still clutched in the other woman's hands. "In the meantime, let's see what else we can find out about what these aliens were up to."

— — —

Kira's stealthed shuttle descended into the atmosphere of the alien world. She took slow, steady breaths inside her powered armor suit, awaiting touchdown.

It went against her training to go in without a set plan, but this mission was also unlike the challenges her team typically faced. An unknown enemy, ambiguous motives, and a mishmash of tech. They could find anything on the world below.

"Stick together. Don't do anything stupid," Kira told her team over the comm. It didn't need to be said, but her role as the team leader dictated she say something.

"We're on high alert," Nia replied. She patted her sidearm.

"I'm patched into the comms and visual feeds, so reach out to me if you need assistance," Jasmine added on the comm.

The shuttle bumped as it landed. Artificial gravity disengaged as the craft powered down, and Kira rose easily from her seat. Scans had shown the gravity to be at approximately 0.6g, so they wouldn't be able to get too crazy, but they'd certainly be able to cover distance much faster than normal.

When the back hatch opened, Kira got her first glimpse of the alien landscape. It had the elements she'd expect to see on a world—groundcover, shrubs, trees, water—but it was devoid of movement. No animals, insects, or even wind.

<*This place comes off as creepily artificial,*> Kira commented to her AI.

<*The suit isn't picking up any distinct heat signatures, though there is a trace of the same ambient radiation we observed throughout this system in space.*>

<*So, that's a 'no' on probable life signs?*>

<*Correct.*>

<*What about that vegetation stuff?*>

<*You'll need to inspect it more closely to be sure.*>

Kira gathered her gear and activated the stealth on her powered armor; her team did likewise. "All right, let's see what we're working with."

Ari took a cautious step toward the rear ramp. "I have absolutely no basis for this remark, but I feel the need to warn against robotic tentacle monsters."

Nia peered outside. "Normally, I'd tell you you're full of it. This time, that warning seems oddly appropriate."

Kyle laughed behind his opaque faceplate. "I'm so playing back this clip the next time one of you rags on me for saying something dumb."

Ari bristled. "Hey, robotic tentacle monsters can be a real menace."

"I'll be on the lookout." Kyle patted his teammate on the shoulder as he passed by.

Kira followed them down the ramp and onto the alien soil. The chartreuse sky enhanced the otherworldly appearance of the place, almost like the planet was in permanent sunset.

"I don't like it," she said to her team.

Nia looked around. "Yeah, it doesn't feel right. It's…" she faded out.

"It's that it's not alive," Ari completed for her.

"Just… sterile." Kyle agreed.

Kira surveyed the surroundings. "It's weirder to see in person than I expected."

"What about that forest?" Nia pointed at the strange trees along the neighboring ridge.

Kira nodded. "Let's check it out." She set a brisk pace toward the trees.

The groundcover was unlike anything Kira had set foot on before. Though it appeared to be moss-covered dirt from a distance, it didn't compress like natural materials. After walking several paces, Kira bent down to inspect it.

She zoomed in and analyzed the dull green material with the sensors on her powered armor. The view on her HUD displayed a mesh of interwoven artificial fibers.

"This just keeps getting more bizarre," she muttered.

Kyle crouched down next to her. "Was all of this manufactured?"

"I have no idea," she replied. "But I'm not excited to meet whoever or whatever could construct an artificial landscape on this scale."

Nia frowned. "Think the entire planet is like this?"

"It all looked the same on scan," Kira said with a shrug. "I don't see why it wouldn't be."

"Does it matter?" Ari continued forward. "We're going after the source of the signal you identified."

Kira nodded. "Right."

Following their discovery of the planet, Aleya and Rodrick had been able to narrow the source of the signal to a valley, adjacent to the site where the shuttle had touched down. They had considered traveling to the exact location, but thick tree cover made the possibility of landing difficult, and they also didn't know what they'd find. For caution's sake, it seemed worthwhile to take a longer walk.

It was easy-going over the terrain, between the light gravity and the powered armor. Kira had to rein in her movements to avoid lunging ahead at an unsafe pace, in case they encountered any hostiles.

At the top of the ridge, she held up her fist, signaling her team to pause. They each took up position behind a tree that afforded a view of the valley beyond.

The aerial survey hadn't done the location justice. Rather than a continuous, thick forest, the landscape on the other side of the ridge was interrupted by an odd outcropping of rocks. The dark stones jutted from the ground in a grooved half-arch that tapered to a narrow tip.

"It's like an ocean storm froze," Nia murmured into her comm.

"That's definitely stone," Kira observed, looking at the density reading displayed on her HUD.

"What would make rock take that kind of shape?" Ari asked.

"Was it grown?" Kyle posited.

"That would fit with the rest of the place," Kira realized.

The trees, the groundcover, the dirt—they all had the same markers of a manufactured substance. It was more likely that the structures had been forced in place rather than each element having been created elsewhere and then arranged. It would take an extreme mastermind to design such a large-scale project, but the Trols may very well have been up to that challenge.

One significant question stood out to Kira. "Where did the raw materials come from for this?" she asked her team.

"The Gaelon System does not appear to have the necessary elements in the natural composition to support construction on this scale," Jasmine stated over the shared comm link.

"Mysar and Elusia, maybe?" Nia speculated.

"It would explain why Reya had infiltrated so many organizations," Kira agreed. "Let's take some samples and see if we can get a match. Really, it doesn't matter where it came from; it's here now."

"Good point." Kyle bent down to gather some material from the ground.

Kira scraped off a sample of the artificial bark from the tree closest to her.

When the samples had been gathered, Kira and her team stored the canisters in slots within their armor. Kira then motioned them forward through the trees. She felt a little ridiculous darting from tree to tree while they were already in stealth gear, but there was no way to know if hidden enemies might be waiting for an opportunity to shoot at them.

When they were halfway down the hillside, Kira signaled for her team to stop. "Do you see a building up there?" She enhanced the view on her HUD and sent the image to her teammates.

The three soldiers evaluated it.

"That does look more squared off than the other rocks," Kyle concurred.

"In all fairness, the forest is laid out on a grid," Kira added. "Still, the color and texture is different than everything around it."

"Huh," Kyle said cryptically.

Kira glanced in his direction. "What?"

"Look at the aerial of this valley with an overlay of the on-the-ground details." Kyle sent the team the composite image. "Look like anything familiar?"

Kira's brow knitted. "A transmission dish."

The strange, curved rocks in the center were positioned at the focal point, and trees filled the main body of the dish. Rock cliffs ringed the outer lip.

"I can't believe I didn't see that before." Kira's stomach knotted. *This is the source of their control.*

"How do we blow it up?" Ari asked.

"This is a *recon* mission," Kira reiterated, though she didn't disagree with the sentiment.

"Let's not kid ourselves," Kyle cut in. "We're totally going to end up blowing this thing to bits. We may as well find its inevitable weakness on this go-around to save ourselves trouble in the future."

"Planning ahead, and all," Nia added.

"You bring up a valid point." Kira sighed. "Let's get a closer look."

They continued down the hillside until they reached the perimeter of the rock formation. Smaller trees were scattered amid the rocks, which explained how they had missed the now-obvious formation when they'd initially looked at it. Kira had learned long before that patterns often didn't emerge until there was some idea of what to look for.

"Whoa, radiation spike," Nia said, breaking the comm silence during the second half of their walk.

"The signal is definitely stronger here, too," Kyle commented.

Kira sensed a pressure in her head. *<Any explanation for*

that?> she asked Jasmine.

<There seems to be a resonance with the neural structure Leon's team dubbed the 'TR'. It's not connected to the signal, but the operating frequencies are similar enough that you're getting feedback, of sorts.>

<This would activate me, though, if I had that other version of the TR?>

<Yes, I think so,> Jasmine confirmed. *<You aren't in any danger. Let me see if I can compensate for the feedback.>*

The pressure in her head diminished.

<Is that better?>

<Much, thank you.> Kira smiled. *<It's nice having you along, Jasmine.>*

<Happy to be of service.>

The team approached the apparent structure at the center of the rock ring.

"That, ladies and gentlemen, is a door," Ari observed.

Sure enough, a door a little over three meters tall and one meter wide was positioned in the center of the structure's nearest side. There was no obvious way to open the door, but an access panel was positioned next to it.

"Want me to get us inside?" Kyle asked.

"Hold for a minute. I need to check in with Sandren," Kira replied. "We're going a little beyond our planned mission scope."

She activated the comm link in her armor and set it to a private channel to connect with the *Raven*.

Sandren answered after five seconds. "What do you make of it, Captain?"

"It's every bit as strange as we observed from above and so much more, sir."

"I'd say I'm glad to hear it, but I'm not sure. I've been

following along on the video feed, and I don't like the look of that structure."

"Neither do I, but it's located at the center of the target site. Seeing the valley up close, the details look strikingly like a transmission dish. None of us saw it from orbit."

"Think that structure is the control center?" Sandren asked.

"Maybe. The question is, do we go inside?"

The major was silent for several seconds. "Do you have enough information about the dwarf planet to recommend a course of action?"

"No, sir."

"Would going inside that building offer additional insights?"

Kira took a slow breath. "Most likely."

"Then you know what you need to do," he stated. "You have your authorization to proceed."

"Yes, sir."

"And Kira," Sandren added after a moment, "watch your backs."

"Always, sir. We'll check in as soon as we have additional information."

She ended the private call and then switched back to her team's channel. "All right, we're going in."

CHAPTER 10

"KYLE AND NIA, can you get that door open?" Kira asked.

"Psh." Kyle snorted. "You needn't even ask."

Kira smiled. "Work your magic."

The two soldiers got to work doing what they did best while Kira and Ari kept watch. The sensors on her suit were unable to penetrate the walls of the structure, so they'd have to wait to see what was inside.

"You know, I would have expected them to make a move to snatch you by now," Ari commented privately to Kira.

"I kind of did, too, actually," she admitted. "As much as I'd like to think our stealth tech makes us invisible, I suspect it's useless against this particular opponent."

"They can probably pick up our specific brainwaves or something."

"That wouldn't surprise me at all." Kira's hand instinctually gravitated toward her sidearm. "We'll need to be extra careful inside. Secret underground lairs are the perfect hiding place for robotic monsters with tentacle arms."

Ari chuckled. "True."

"This motherfoker," Kyle swore into the comm.

"I haven't seen encryption this intense outside of the Guard." Nia sighed.

"Can you break it?" Kira asked, switching back over to the team's common band.

"Of course." Kyle swore again under his breath. "It's just going to take a little time."

After four minutes of cycling through their various hacking tricks, Kyle and Nia eventually found a combination that worked.

"Take that, Trol bastards!" Kyle exclaimed as the door hissed open.

"If that was their front door, I can't imagine what the computer systems are going to be like," Nia said with far less enthusiasm.

"Another point that I hesitate to even mention," Kira began, "is why there's a door and a panel that resembles the tech we're used to. I can justify building a planet with the same organic composition and general habitat that we're used to as Tarans, but a structure like this…"

"Yep, just going to choose to ignore that point for now." Ari readied his multi-handgun and stepped through the open doorway.

As he entered, lights came on.

"Okay, yep, the stealth tech is pointless," he said.

Kira could make out, around Ari's shoulders, what appeared to be some sort of control room with desks and monitors. She followed him inside to get a better look.

The room was laid out with three computer stations along the wall, complete with an array of monitors, and a door similar to the entry point positioned on the left wall. Again, her suit's sensors only read as far as the room.

"I'm going to guess that's the way in," she commented. She checked her suit's settings and saw that the signal to the *Raven* was cutting in and out. "Ah, shite."

Nia must have noticed the same thing. "We're going to be in the dark, aren't we?"

"Looks like it." Kira sighed. "One sec." She stepped back outside to warn Sandren that their connection would likely be severed as soon as they entered the underground facility. He instructed them to proceed, offering additional words of caution.

When Kira got back inside, she found Kyle and Nia each working at one of the computer terminals. The screens above the desktops displayed what looked like scrolling gibberish.

"This won't be easy," Nia stated without taking her eyes off the screen in front of her.

"I'm trying to find a root database, but this isn't laid out like a normal system," Kyle added. "And this coding is weird. I'm going to try running it through the external processor." He pulled out one of his specialized pieces of equipment—a small black box that contained powerful software that advanced Lynaedan AI had helped design to interface with encrypted computer operating systems.

Kyle dropped beneath the desk to look for wires to use as a hard jack into the alien computer. "If I can't make sense of this, we're out of luck."

"I think I may have found the door controls, at least," Nia said.

"Bomax, I was kind of hoping we'd have to blow it up," Ari replied.

Kira rolled her eyes. "Yes, explosives near the computers is a *great* idea."

<Kira, perhaps I can assist Kyle and Nia,> Jasmine offered.

<If you want to try, be my guest. I just don't want to have to brain jack into this system.>

<I can connect wirelessly to Kyle's external processor. If I do so, though, it will require most of my resources. While I'm distracted, I'm afraid you may feel some physical effects like you experienced earlier.>

<Go for it. I can take it.>

A moment later, the pressure she had felt in her head when they first stepped into the rock formation returned twofold, and this time it was accompanied by a high-pitched buzzing that stabbed behind her eyes. "Argh!"

"You okay over there?" Ari asked.

"Yeah, just don't ask me to do math or be patient with children for a few minutes." Kira placed one gloved hand on the side of her helmet while she breathed deeply.

"Jasmine, you're a genius!" Kyle cheered after a minute.

"This is, indeed, a strange system," Jasmine said over the team's suit comms. "I noticed that the frequency being emitted from the transmitter has a visual wave pattern similar to the arrangement of geographic features on this world. I extrapolated that layout to the computer system architecture, and it matched. The database is located at a system core analogous to the location of this facility relative to the rest of the world."

Kira scowled. "I didn't follow all of that, but it sounds like you found what you're looking for."

"Yes," Jasmine confirmed.

"Good. We'll go with that."

Kira waited while her team followed through on Jasmine's lead. The pressure in her head remained, but after a couple of minutes she found herself getting used to it.

"Ah ha!" Nia let out a delighted cackle. "Got it cornered now."

"Shite, this is going to take forever to download over the slow connection through this firewall," Kyle groaned.

The hum in Kira's head diminished as Jasmine disconnected from the external processor. *<Sorry to have put you through that.>*

<I've experienced a lot worse than a headache.>

<Glad it wasn't too bad,> the AI replied. *<We were able to find the data repository, but we don't have the storage capacity on hand to hold all of it. I set up a crawler to extract information related to the Elvar Trinary. It'll take at least an hour to comb through and copy the relevant data.>*

<Do you need to be here for that?> Kira asked.

<Actively monitoring the transfer from this room? No.>

<Then how about we go check out what's underground while it finishes?>

Jasmine gave a mental scowl. *<The data will likely offer insights into what's going on down there. It's prudent to wait until we know what we're up against.>*

<Or, countermeasures against our presence on this world might trigger at any moment, and we could lose out on our only opportunity to investigate,> Kira pointed out.

<By that token, we may all die.>

<You really know how to spread the cheer, Jasmine.>

<I'm not joking. It's certain to be dangerous down there.>

<We knew that when we came in here,> Kira reminded the AI. *<Remember what we discussed about life in the Guard? We run toward the danger, not away from it.>*

Jasmine made the mental equivalent of a harrumph. *<Suit yourself.>*

<Wow, you are temperamental for an AI!>

<You're not the only one with adjustments to make, Kira.

I'm used to being safely tucked away in a lab.>

<Suck it up. We'll get through this.> Kira returned her attention to her team. "All right. Sounds like it's going to take some time to copy the data, so let's check out the facility and leave this running up here."

Ari shifted on his feet. "That's assuming we exit the same way we go in."

"Worst case, this entry isn't far from our original landing location in the shuttle. We can always circle back here if needed," Kira replied.

Kyle nodded. "I don't really want to wait around here watching a progress bar march across the screen. I vote for exploration time."

Kira's statement hadn't been an open call for votes, but she decided to let it slide. "Get that door open," she ordered.

"And... presto." Nia made an entry on her computer terminal.

A bolt clanged, and the door popped open with a hiss. It slowly swung inward.

There was only darkness beyond, and the sensors feeding into her HUD indicated a featureless corridor with uniform temperature. A row of lights along the ceiling illuminated, and strips along the floor to either side of the corridor lit the path to an apparent stairwell.

"Oh yeah, absolutely nothing ominous about that," Ari said.

Kira swallowed, happy her opaque helmet hid her face. "Nothing to worry about." She hoped her tone sounded more confident than she felt.

Before her team could reply, she strode forward through the open doorway, her multi-handgun aimed ahead.

Ari followed. "Let me go first, ma'am. If they're after you, you should stay in between us."

The idea of being literally snatched from the group hadn't occurred to her, but if it made Ari feel better to go first, there was no reason to stop him. "Go ahead," she consented.

Ari slipped past her in the corridor to scope out the stairwell ahead. "I can't see past the first switchback."

"We'll take it slow," Kira instructed. "Hopefully it's not too deep."

It was.

The stone stairwell descended twenty-four stories, with flights of twelve steps each forming one side of a spiraling square around a solid central column. With each floor, Kira was reminded how strange it was that there were *stairs* on this alien world. Person-sized stairs. Not to mention twenty-four stories and no elevator. Nothing about the place added up.

"This is really foking weird, right?" Kira said as they rounded the second switchback of the twenty-fourth story.

"Oh, without a doubt," Ari agreed.

"Whoever this architect was, they're fired," Nia joked.

"Wouldn't that be more of a structural engineer?" Kyle asked.

"They'd do the load ratings on the stairs," Nia replied, "but I think it'd be an architect who'd make the call between a stairwell versus an elevator."

Ari stopped short in front of Kira. "We're here."

Kira peeked around the last bend and saw a metal door in front of Ari—unmarked and with no window or accompanying control panel. She tried to get a reading of the space beyond, but the same interference she'd experienced on the surface prevented her suit's sensors from penetrating the walls.

<We won't be able to make a very quick exit from here,> Jasmine cautioned.

<Leave the military protocol to me. Just keep me from

turning into a Robus, or having a seizure, and we'll be good.>

Kira focused on the door. "Is it unlocked?"

Ari pushed on it, and the door swung inward.

"You first." Kira used her right arm to swing the door wide while Ari rushed in to assess the interior with his weapon drawn.

"Clear," he announced. "I mean, there's nothing to see."

With the door open, Kira's HUD completed the map of the other side. Another long corridor stretched ahead. This time, though, the walls showed a heat signature—and were pulsing in temperature from warm to hot every three seconds.

"Ummm…" She waited for her team to offer additional commentary.

"Please tell me we aren't about to walk down the esophagus of some giant space monster," Nia said from two steps up the stairwell.

"And all of you laughed at me before." Ari shook his head.

"It's not a circulatory pulse," Kyle observed. "I bet you these are cables relaying data bursts. They heat up when the signal passes through and diffuse the heat into the stone in between the bursts—keeps it from overheating and melting."

"The signal for telepathic control?" Kira asked.

The soldier nodded. "That would be my guess."

"Where's the origin point?" Nia asked. "The cables have to run somewhere."

Ari pointed ahead with his handgun. "Only one way forward."

Kira tried to suppress the disquiet nagging at the back of her mind. *They wanted me, and this is a place designed for my people. It can't be a coincidence.*

The team advanced down the corridor for another hundred meters before an exit was visible up ahead.

"There's a larger chamber," Ari observed. "More than one, I think."

The end of the corridor fanned outward until it blended with the smooth walls of a domed chamber twenty meters tall and twice as many wide. Three other corridor entrances, identical to the one they'd traversed, were positioned at equidistant points around the base of the walls. In the center of the space, a bundle of thick cables funneled into a rock formation that resembled the wave forms on the surface, only with the arches curving outward from the structure like petals of a blooming flower.

"Yeah, I'm at a complete loss," Kira admitted.

<Oh, that's interesting.>

<See something, Jasmine?>

<Your suit couldn't get clear readings of the rocks on the surface, between the ambient radiation and the other structures. There's a high enough concentration here, though, and the analysis is quite intriguing.>

<Which is...?> Kira couldn't keep the impatience out of her mental tone. The science-minded AI's approach to gather sufficient data and offering context for every statement didn't quite mesh with Kira's shoot-as-soon-as-you-know-they're-the-bad-guys approach.

<The mineral in this rock is the same ateron-like substance that's in the TRs. Leon's team started referring to it in their research notes as 'valteron'.>

<Oh, shite.> Kira's pulse spiked. "Jasmine just clued me in that these rocks are made of the same material as the telepathic receptors they discovered in my brain and in the subverted people."

"Fok, really?" Kyle eyed the rocks. "I guess it makes sense to use the same substance in the transmitter."

Kira nodded. "Leon's team is calling it 'valteron'—presumably because of the Valta connection and similarity to ateron."

Ari shrugged. "Makes sense."

"But, we're still missing a critical piece here—we have the transmission equipment, but where is the signal coming from? Where are the Trols?" Nia questioned.

"I have no idea." Kira looked around, but there were still no signs of life. "Let's check out the other corridors."

They cautiously made their way across the chamber. Though Kyle and Nia tried to remotely interface with the computer system, they couldn't find a signal compatible with their suits. With the external processor still up in the control room—or whatever it was—at the surface, they had no other way to access the system. The best option was to do a visual inspection and see what information they could gather the old fashioned way.

The first corridor on the right terminated forty meters down at a stone monument, which resembled a miniature version of the structure in the center of the main chamber. Cables disappeared into the stone ceiling, and there were no other signs indicating the structure's purpose or if it extended beyond what was visible in the corridor.

The second corridor mirrored the first, though when they reached the end, there wasn't a stairwell; instead, there was a pit.

The team's HUDs indicated a potential tripping hazard up ahead, and they slowed their pace as they approached.

"What is it?" Kira frowned at the dark nothingness two meters in front of her.

The round pit was roughly ten meters across. Its walls were the same stone found elsewhere in the facility, but it resembled natural stone more than the smooth, concrete-like finish on many of the floors and walls. No wind or sound came from the opening. Its only distinguishing feature was that the temperature increased the deeper the hole went—until the sensors cut out at approximately three hundred meters. At that depth, there was still no sign of the bottom.

"I didn't think this could possibly get any weirder, but mission accomplished," Nia stated. She took a step back from the pit.

Ari craned his neck over the edge. "There's no way we can get down there."

"If we had a kilometer of cordage we could," Kira said. "But seeing that we don't, it'll have to wait." She turned to go.

"You came to us," a chorus of raspy voices said in her mind.

Fok! Her pulse spiked. *<Jasmine, did you hear that?>*

<No, Kira, what is it?>

<A voice—voices. They were...> She listened for more, and then ventured a mental call. *"Hello?"*

There was no reply.

<The main reason we're on this mission is so you can try to connect with them,> Jasmine said in her mind.

<I know.> Kira took a slow breath and cleared her mind. *"We'd like to speak with you,"* she telepathically called out to the voices. *"We don't want to be enemies."*

Silence.

Kira sighed. *<This isn't working.>*

<You're not trying very hard.>

<Forgive me for not being very enthusiastic about getting buddy-buddy after what they did to me.> Kira turned away from the pit. "Let's get out of here," she told her team.

"Don't need to ask me twice," Nia hurried away.

When they were ten meters away, Kira addressed her team.

"I didn't want to say anything by the pit, but I made contact with the Trols. Briefly. They said, 'You came to us'. A chorus of them."

Ari tensed. "Were they... down there?"

"I don't *know!*" Kira took a shaky breath. "Maybe they're *everywhere*. These beings aren't like anything we've dealt with before. They don't seem to have bodies."

"Why aren't we running for the door?" Nia asked.

"Because we haven't completed our investigation. Hearing those voices was disconcerting, but we always figured they'd be watching us. And I'm *supposed* to be trying to communicate with them. Until they take physical action to harm us, we proceed."

"If and when they act, it'll already be too late," Ari replied.

<He's right. We should leave now,> Jasmine advised.

Kira continued undeterred. *<We haven't checked out the last corridor.>*

<You're in danger.>

<We don't have enough information to draw a definitive conclusion about this place. Getting a creepy vibe isn't enough to order a military strike. We need evidence of a weapon if we're going to get support to take this thing out for good.>

<You're willing to die to serve as evidence of danger?> the AI asked.

<If I have to. That's part of the job.>

While it wasn't a reality Kira was eager to face, she accepted the risks that came with her position. And, if the aliens wanted her, she'd gladly sacrifice herself to save the rest of her team.

"The rest of you should head back to the surface," Kira stated. "I'll scope out the last corridor and then meet you up there."

"Leave you here alone with them?" Ari shook his head. "No

way."

"You stay, we all stay," Kyle agreed.

Nia reluctantly nodded her head.

"Fine, but at the first sign of trouble, you run. Don't worry about me," Kira instructed.

"With all due respect, ma'am, that's our call to make," Kyle said as he passed by her.

Kira sighed, but the sentiment warmed her heart. She would've said the same thing in his shoes.

They retraced their steps and then crossed through the central chamber to the final unexplored corridor, to the left where they'd first entered. The space was immediately a stark contrast to the areas they'd encountered elsewhere.

Notably, there were rooms. The surroundings reminded Kira of a less polished version of the MTech lab on Valta, with doors along long corridors and windows looking into labs and medical rooms. The details were missing from this place to make it a direct comparison, but something about it kept jogging her memory.

"I think there might be another way down here," Kyle said.

"What makes you say that?" Kira asked him.

"If these rooms are ever supposed to be occupied, it doesn't make sense to bring in people via that stairwell. I bet the far end of this hall leads to another exit."

Ari shrugged. "One way to find out."

"If there's a more direct way out of here, I'm all for it," Nia agreed.

They continued down the central corridor, which branched to various side passageways servicing other labs and storage areas. Their suits' sensors mapped the corridors that weren't obstructed by a sealed door, and their HUDs updated to display a labyrinth spanning thousands of square meters.

Nia groaned as the HUD refreshed with a new branch of hallways. "There's no way we can go through all of this right now."

"Hopefully the data you're downloading will shed some light on the purpose of this place," Kira replied.

Kyle scoffed. "Pretty sure its singular aim is to keep us guessing."

Kira tightened the grip on her weapon. "Maybe that's the key. We keep talking about *what* we're seeing, but what about going to the underlying *why*? What were the Trols after?"

"Well," Nia began, "we know they were in league with the Mysarans."

"I guess that would explain why there are person-sized corridors here, and a breathable atmosphere," Kira said. "Still, why would beings that can project their consciousness across light years need a bunch of Tarans?"

Ari frowned. "You said they feed on negative emotional energy, right?"

"They at least need it to maintain control of their host," Kira replied.

"Starting a civil war would be a good way to get people in a bad mood," Kyle pointed out.

"They did go to great lengths to pit Elusia and Mysar against each other," Nia agreed.

Kyle nodded. "Yeah. And MTech had a bunch of armor and weapons stashed in the lab, right, Kira?"

"Yes, but that part doesn't make sense," Kira responded. "I get that the Robus were supposed to be soldiers to fight on Mysar's behalf, but their physical modifications would make it difficult to use conventional weapons."

"Not to be Mr. Contrary over here," Ari interjected, "but how closely did you look at the rifles you found?"

"I was a little distracted by trying to not get caught," Kira admitted. "Why?"

"You should probably see this for yourself." Ari gestured toward a chest-height window in the wall.

Her stomach knotting, Kira walked over and looked inside. "Oh, fok."

The window overlooked a storeroom containing racks of rifles. Unlike the weapons Kira had used throughout her career, these had no hand grip or trigger.

"No…"

"It looks like these would mount directly to the armor, likely with a mental control chip for firing," Ari completed for her. "These soldiers of theirs were designed for nasty killing, end of story."

It's wrong on so many levels. Kira tore her gaze away from the storeroom. "Why not just drop a bomb at that point, for such indiscriminate destruction?"

Nia's face looked pale. "Because it's not about who's getting attacked. It's about the *suffering* on both sides."

Kira's stomach dropped. "Shite, you're right." She shook her head. "I kept looking at it from a Taran vantage—what they'd have to gain, what they're working toward. But no. We're just like food to them."

"And now they're getting ready for the harvest," Ari murmured.

"How very poetic." Nia gripped her handgun a little tighter.

Kyle scowled. "No, we're missing something. Why go through the effort to develop Robus?"

"Maximum killing potential equals maximum suffering inflicted?" Kira speculated.

"Not buying it," Kyle said. "This is a race that can construct an artificial planet. They must have a larger play than watching a single system tear itself apart through civil war."

"Whatever their aim, we've learned what we came here to find out," Kira continued. "It's clear they mean harm, and this facility is where they mean to bring soldiers to retrofit them into killing machines."

"Time to go?" Nia asked eagerly.

Kira nodded. "Yeah, come on." She turned to head back in the direction they'd come from.

"What about locating the alternate exit?" Ari reminded her.

"Oh, right." It wasn't like her to forget a lead like that.

<You have a lot on your mind. Don't be too hard on yourself,> Jasmine soothed.

<You're just happy because we're finally getting out of here.>

<Like you aren't?>

That was true. "Mapping out that exit sounds like a great excuse to avoid going through that center chamber again," Kira told her team.

Nia picked up her pace in the direction of the suspected exit. "I was hoping you'd say that."

"Wow, Nia, you *really* don't like it down here." Kira chuckled.

"How are you even remotely okay with this place?" the lance corporal shot back. "You said yourself that there were alien voices taunting you in your head."

"Jasmine's keeping me in a happy place," Kira replied. *<What you're doing isn't impairing my judgment, is it?>*

<I've tried to keep my interventions to a minimum while alleviating the discomfort from the interference,> the AI replied.

<It didn't occur to me that I should be more concerned than

I feel. Like when you told me before that we should go and I insisted that we stay.>

<Well, we're leaving now. That's the important part,> Jasmine stated.

<We'll need to have Doctor Elric look over my medical logs when we get back to headquarters to make sure everything is okay.>

<Good plan,> the AI agreed.

Ari led the team along the path he'd mapped out toward the likely alternative exit point.

Based on Kira's own evaluation of the map, his guess looked sound. Most of the corridors seemed to feed into one central pathway, which extended the full length of the map their suit sensors had been able to populate. The far end, however, appeared to terminate in a shielded door.

<Either a trap or the exit,> Kira said privately to Jasmine.

<Please be an exit!>

Ari was the first to reach the barrier. "It's locked."

Kyle joined him by the control panel next to the door. "We have the encryption protocol saved from before. This shouldn't take long."

He synced with the panel and input the necessary commands. The door bolt slid open with a satisfying *clang*, which was followed by the hiss of the seal releasing.

The two men braced on either side of the door with their weapons pointed ahead. Kira took up position next to Ari, with Nia on the other side by Kyle.

To their relief, only an empty, four-meter-wide tunnel was waiting for them on the other side.

Nia lowered her weapon. "You know, after our experiences over the last couple of weeks, it's really nice to walk through an entire facility and not get shot at."

Kyle groaned. "Fok, Nia, now you've jinxed us."

"We're not out of here until we're out of here," Ari reminded them.

Kira nodded. "Don't let your guard down."

They forged ahead.

The floor sloped upward at a shallow angle suitable for transporting materials on a hover cart. Kira expected it to switch back on itself and exit somewhere close to the control room, but their HUDs showed the trajectory was a straight shot for eight hundred fifty meters ahead.

Thanks to the low gravity, the team was able to lope up the hill and cover the distance quickly. Kira kept watch on the shadows playing on the rough stone walls of the tunnel.

They slowed their pace as they neared the end.

Kira paused to look back down the tunnel while the others continued ahead. The lights had turned off down in the lab area where they'd come from.

She turned back to face her team. "All right, let's see where this dumps us out. Then we can circle back to the control room to retrieve that data drive."

Kyle nodded. "Sounds good—"

"Shite!" Ari shouted.

Kira's jaw dropped. The tunnel walls that had seemed solid only seconds before were now a swirling mass of particulates.

"Run!"

CHAPTER 11

KIRA RACED FORWARD through the flurry of sand-like particles. "What the fok is this?!"

"I'll make sure our exit is clear. Get Kira!" Kyle surged ahead.

Ari and Nia tried to get back to her three meters behind them in the tunnel, but the particles bound together to form a lattice barrier in their path.

Ari struck it with his arm. The latticework flexed to accommodate the blow. "Sneaky bastards waited until the rest of us were at the exit," he spat.

The particles glommed onto Kira's powered armor and attempted to stick her boots to the floor. She trudged forward, but each step was more labored than the last as the particles congealed around her. After four steps, she may as well have been walking through hip-deep cement.

"It's got me!" she shouted.

"I already hate these things." Nia readied her multi-handgun on the sonic setting. "Mute your suit," she instructed Kira.

Jasmine completed the action for her.

Nia fired three blasts. The particles shuddered as the high-powered sound wave passed over them, but the latticework remained intact.

I need to be stronger! I need to break free.

The Robus within Kira stirred, begging to be let out. Her mind felt clearer and sharper than it had since they landed on the world. So much power was right at her fingertips.

<Kira! I sense you're about to shift,> Jasmine warned.

<Let me! It may be the boost I need.>

<You can't!> the AI pleaded. *<The helmet can't accommodate the transformation. If you shift, it'll break the seal, and those particles could get inside you.>*

Kira tried to hold back, but her pulse was quickening. The power called to her. *<You need to stop it, Jasmine!>*

<I'm trying!>

The sweet call to transform began to fade.

Kira looked down in horror to see what looked like stone solidifying around her feet and shins. She couldn't take another step.

<I need another way to break free!>

<Maybe a concussive blast,> Jasmine suggested.

"Kinetics!" Kira shouted over the comm to her team. She managed to get her multi-handgun in position and started firing at her feet.

Ari joined with Nia in unloading a magazine at her legs.

Impacts registered on Kira's HUD as the suit absorbed the fire.

<It's loosening.> Kira managed to swing one leg forward. *<Jasmine, can you do anything?>*

<I'll override the automatic stop points on the servos. It'll boost your power.>

Kira sensed a shift in the controls as she took another step.

The next came easier as she gained some momentum. "Find out where we are. Get the shuttle!" she ordered.

"Already in progress," Kyle replied.

Ari and Nia continued firing well-placed shots around Kira's feet to keep the particles from regaining a hold of her.

"Stay, Kira," a voice beckoned inside her head. *"This is where you belong."*

"Leave me the fok alone!" She blocked out the aliens' calls, focusing on each step to the exit.

She made it to Ari and Nia's position.

"Get her outside, Nia," Ari said.

He took up the rear while Nia and Kira cut through the path Kyle was helping to keep clear from the outside.

The tunnel exited into a small clearing in the forest. A rock cliff towered behind them, but it was no longer solid stone; particles swirled above the surface.

"Shite! Is this entire place going to come after us?" Kira checked her multi-handgun and saw that she was on her last magazine of kinetic rounds.

"We're two kilometers away from the landing site. Pod will be here in a minute," Kyle reported.

They'd need more than bullets to make it that long, if the entire cliff face disintegrated.

"Hold them off!" Kira grabbed her plasma rifle off her back and sent a spray of fire across the sky.

The particles glowed red for an instant as the plasma passed over them, and then they dropped to the ground as blacked specks.

Over the tree canopy, Kira spotted the shuttle approaching.

"Take off as soon as we're all on board. We're getting out of here!"

"What about the data drive?" Nia asked.

"Forget it. I have all the evidence I need that this place is hostile." Kira sprayed her plasma fire into the swarm of particles, hoping to keep clear a large enough area for the shuttle to land.

The swarm gathered around the shuttle as it descended, coalescing into chains that extended toward the ground.

"Little fokers think they can tether it!" Ari shot at one of the chains.

"Get inside." Kira ran for the back hatch as soon as it dropped open. "There's no way they're stronger than the engine."

The team piled into the shuttle while trying to hold off as many of the particles as they could. When everyone was inside, Kira slammed her hand on the button next to the door to close it.

Kyle dove to the cockpit and activated the liftoff.

"Shite, some of them are inside!" Nia flailed her arms in a vain attempt to shake them off.

"Get us off the ground!" Kira urged Kyle.

The shuttle rocketed upward a second later.

Kira looked out the viewport and saw that the swarm hadn't been able to keep up with the shuttle.

"Everyone strap in," she instructed.

They all took their seats and secured the harness. As soon as everyone was ready, Kira hit the door control to open the back hatch.

Intense wind ripped through the craft's interior, rippling the belts and anything with a loose end. The little particles didn't stand a chance.

Kira left the hatch open for thirty seconds, but she was forced to close it when the shuttle reached the upper level of the artificial planet's atmosphere. There could be some particles in the craft but not enough to do any damage.

"Message the *Raven* that we'll need to go through decontamination procedures," Kira instructed. "I don't want to take any risks that these things can replicate."

"Aye," Kyle acknowledged.

"That was really close." Nia let out a long breath and slouched in her seat.

<That was quick thinking, Kira. Well done,> Jasmine praised.

<It's not just my hide on the line anymore. Glad we both got out of there.>

The AI was silent for a moment. *<Leaving that external processor is a problem.>*

<The data—>

<It's not about what we were extracting. It's what the Trols get. There's a sophisticated firewall around the drive that would take even the most sophisticated intelligence at least six hours to crack. Hooking up for an hour or two for a data transfer is fine, but leaving it there indefinitely opens the possibility for the Trols to learn about our most advanced algorithms.>

Kira's heart dropped. *<Jasmine! Why didn't you have me go back for it?>*

<Because I extrapolated the potential scenarios and determined that once we were under attack, we would not be able to retrieve the device and make it off the planet. We could have gone back for it, but we would have been stranded. Either way, the drive would remain on the world. The option we pursued at least got the people out.>

<We need to go back!>

<That task would have no chance of success with your current loadout. Regroup on the Raven *with Sandren and assess*

the options.>

Kira slumped in her seat. *This may be the biggest mistake I've ever made.*

They rode the rest of the way to the *Raven* in silence.

After the shuttle docked, the vessel and the team underwent a thorough decontamination and nanoscopic scan to make sure all particles had been removed. Several hundred were found in crevasses within the shuttle and powered armor, and the samples were promptly incinerated.

Once cleared, Kira and her team went up to the residential level to meet with Sandren.

He was waiting for them in the galley. "What happened down there?" Despite his sharp tone, his expression was one of fatherly concern.

"I feel like we simultaneously know more and less about what we're up against, sir," Kira began. She filled him in on the events leading up to their hasty retreat.

"What a shiteshow," Sandren muttered when she was finished.

"Yes, sir, it really is." Kira glanced at her team. "We'd like to make this right. *I* need to."

Sandren crossed his arms. "Well, you weren't able to make contact with them in a meaningful way. That was our main hope—to resolve this conflict in a civil fashion."

"I didn't get the impression they're interested in talking. Reya and Nox sure talked a big game, but the chorus was different." Kira paused. "Huh, I just thought of something. Reya and Nox were paired in a person for an extended time. I wonder if being around Tarans changed them?"

The major tilted his head. "How so?"

"Well, Nox and Reya spoke in Taran terms about their motivations when I interrogated them. And I was able to get inside their minds—maybe that's because they had a frame of reference from their time in a Taran body. They had integrated our biological and social experience into their being, just like the race integrates technology," Kira explained. "But what if I couldn't force a connection with the other beings because they've never been in a form like ours? They didn't have that frame of reference."

"Hmm." Sandren stroked his chin. "How might we go about establishing that common vocabulary?"

"Slow, dedicated outreach."

"We don't have that luxury."

"I know, sir."

Sandren rose from the table. "I'll talk to Kaen. Stand by."

— — —

Waiting for news from field teams was always one of Kaen's least favorite times as a commander. Situations such as this, when so much was on the line, made the waiting that much worse.

He'd tried to keep himself distracted with the various administrative tasks his position demanded, but as the day stretched on, he found his task list looking a little thin.

To his relief, a call from Major Sandren illuminated on his desktop. *Finally!*

"Major, good to hear from you," he greeted. "What news do you have about Gaelon?"

"I wish the report was better. We found a gas giant in the system, and a dwarf planet, which by all measures is an artificial creation," Sandren explained. "Kira and her team went down to the surface, but they were unable to enter into a meaningful discussion with the aliens. They were attacked on their way out, and... we may have a situation."

Kaen braced. "Which is?"

"They were forced to leave behind an external processor."

Fok! Kaen fought to retain composure. "They *left* it there? This race is known to appropriate technology! How could they be so careless?"

"They were under attack. There was no way to go back."

Kaen wiped his hands down his face. "We have no choice but to reformat our entire computer network now."

"That's a drastic move, sir. Kira would like another chance to interface with them."

"If that route had any chance of success, it would have come about on this first visit. No. They could neutralize our defenses at any time. We need to act while we can."

"Yes, sir." Sandren gave a grim nod.

"Get back here to base. We'll figure out our next steps." Kaen severed the connection.

As if these aliens weren't going to be difficult enough to beat. He would have liked the opportunity to learn more about the technology they used, but knowing that the adaptive algorithms on the external processor were now in the aliens possession, there wasn't time to figure out a long-term strategic play. They needed to hit the enemy hard and fast. *If only we had some inside information of our own...*

— — —

Ellen was still agitated after her field trip to the valley. *What are they hiding down there?*

She hated having information dangled in front of her face and not knowing how to interpret it. The records they'd obtained from the facility were a disorganized mess. Only one bit of information stood out to her.

She flipped through the items again on her temporary workstation in the Mysaran government office. The mining records stored at the remote site had to be significant. *But why?*

Ellen looked at the production logs again. Not working in the mining industry, the volume number was meaningless to her in isolation. She brought up a calculator app on her desktop and divided the numbers by days in the year to get a feel for daily output.

She frowned. It seemed like an unusually high volume, but it was entirely possible she was making something out of nothing. To be sure, she dug around in the computer system for the Mysaran annual report from the previous year to look at the GDP metrics.

Her breath caught in her throat. "This can't be right."

She re-checked her math. *Did I get the timeframe wrong?*

When she verified her source data from the valley site, the numbers she'd used for her calculations checked out.

"Trisha, Fiona, come in here, would you?" she called over the comm.

A minute later, the two women arrived from their own offices.

"Yes?" Trisha asked.

"Take a look at this. Am I missing something?" Ellen flipped the information displayed on her desk so they could get a better look.

Fiona frowned. "That can't be right."

Trisha shook her head. "How could mining production be five times more than all the materials used on the entire planet?"

"I was wondering the same thing." Ellen slumped back in her chair.

She could understand production being one, or maybe even two, times Mysar's own consumption, due to trade within the system, but five times... She couldn't even wrap her head around where the labor resources would come from to extract the material.

"I can't find records for what happened to any of the ore," Ellen continued. "It's noted in these logs as being mined, and then it just disappears."

"Material on that scale doesn't just *go away*." Fiona crossed her arms. "Someone is hiding it."

Ellen pointed to the absurd quantity of ore. "Where could anyone possible hide that?"

"In that underground facility, maybe?" Trisha ventured.

"Why pull it out of the ground only to stick it back in the ground elsewhere?" Ellen shook her head. "That doesn't make sense."

"Do you think it was transported offworld?" Fiona asked.

Trisha scowled. "If that's the case, then to where?"

"There is one other place I've heard mentioned in relation to these aliens," Ellen replied, deciding that 'need-to-know' included these two allies. "Gaelon. As challenging as it would be to get the materials over there, it makes more sense than hiding a bunch of ore somewhere on Mysar."

"Gaelon?" Fiona said with a raised eyebrow. "There's nothing in that system."

"Actually, I had always heard it was too dangerous to venture into because of radiation," Trisha countered.

"On Valta, they told us it was a bad place but gave no real explanation," Ellen said. "Needless to say, that's a lot of talk with nothing to substantiate it. Given we were also not told that the Mysaran chancellor was actually an alien puppet, I think it's safe to say that we've been misled over the years."

"I can't argue with that," Fiona conceded.

Trisha nodded. "Now that there's a new source of information, we need to reset our understanding."

"I agree," Ellen said, "which is why I wanted to run this by you. This evidence points to a conspiracy on a scale that's beyond our capability to address on our own."

"Did you find anything else in the data from the facility aside from the mining records?" Fiona asked.

"Perhaps, but I have to admit I'm not sure what I'm looking at. There's a ton of information here, but it looks like it's encrypted somehow—or completely disorganized. I don't know."

Fiona looked over her shoulder. "Something about this is familiar…"

"If the goings on in that place are as messed up as they seem, we need to get the information to someone who can interpret it."

Across the table, Fiona's face paled. "Wait, I know where I've seen this code before! It's what Hale used when she wrote messages to the people we now know were subverted."

Ellen looked up from the desktop. "We need to get this to the Tararian Guard."

CHAPTER 12

I'VE NEVER HAD a mission go so foking wrong, Kira chastised herself while the *Raven* made its final approach to Orion Station.

She'd tried to keep the thought private, but she felt Jasmine pick up on her feelings.

<You were given an impossible task, and your team made it out unharmed. That's the best outcome we could have hoped for,> the AI soothed.

<I never should have allowed them to leave that drive unattended. I know better.>

<It seemed like the right call at the time.>

Kira only shook her head in response.

Sandren had been surprisingly understanding about the situation, but Kira doubted Kaen would be so forgiving. She was already walking a fine line with field ops, following her unexpected upgrade to a Robus, and such a gross error that compromised the Guard's security might tip her over to a desk job—or worse.

Except I'd die in an office post. Though she was sure Leon would be thrilled, it was hardly a deciding factor when she envisioned her future career path.

<*They're not going to bench you,*> Jasmine said.

<*You have no way of knowing that.*>

<*I know enough. You weren't the only one who left that drive there. Kyle and Nia signed off the action, as did I. You don't share the full brunt of that decision.*>

<*But I was in command. I had the final say.*>

<*My report will say you acted in the best interest in the moment. There was no wrongdoing.*>

Kira didn't share the AI's confidence. While Jasmine's endorsement would carry weight when it came to the Guard command's review, it didn't make Kira feel better about herself.

Did the Trols get to me? Or have I just been too distracted by my own issues to focus on the mission the way I should? She didn't have an answer, but thorough med and psych evaluations were in order either way.

The *Raven* docked in its typical berth, and Kira went to grab her travel items from the team's cabin.

"When are we going back there to finish the job?" Nia asked as she grabbed her own bag from her bunk.

"I don't know," Kira replied. "There are a few ways this could go."

"That whole place needs to be destroyed," Ari stated.

"Would that be enough? Who's to say that's all of them?" Kyle countered. "This group has shown themselves to be a threat to us, and they've been unresponsive to our attempts to open a dialogue. We can't just ignore them."

"They're in an unoccupied system. If they don't venture beyond that, maybe it won't matter," Nia said.

Kira shook her head. "No way. They've insinuated

themselves into Taran life once, so they'd do it again."

"Yep, they need to go," Ari reiterated.

"We'll obey whatever direction Kaen gives," Kira stated. She slung her travel bag over her shoulder. "I'll talk to you after my debrief with Sandren and the colonel."

Her team wished her well while they exited via the gangway, and Kira headed straight for Medical.

A nurse directed Kira to Doctor Elric in a back exam room. "How are you feeling, Kira?" the doctor greeted her.

"Good, physically speaking," Kira replied, hopping on the exam bed. "Jasmine was able to counter some negative effects during the op, so it seems to be working out."

The doctor smiled while he initiated a full body scan. "Glad to hear it. I'll take a copy of your records from her and look for anything concerning." He tilted his head. "Is there anything you'd like me to be on the lookout for, in particular?"

"I have no idea what those logs even look like."

"I mean, do you have any concerns about your state? Any incidents of note?"

"Oh." Kira looked down. "I guess, shortly after we arrived on the planet, we went into a formation of rocks that we later determined are made of valteron—the same substance as my TR. I got a bad headache, and Jasmine was able to block it out. The only other thing that's maybe worth mentioning is that I…" she faded out as she sought the right words. "I guess, I didn't feel worried at times like I maybe should have."

"Can you quantify that at all?" Elric asked.

"Not really. And it's not something I noticed at the time. I only bring it up because Nia asked me at one point why I wasn't running for the door. Aside from when I almost shifted while we were in battle, I was perfectly calm. I feel like I should have at least been… unnerved when we were walking around."

"All right, I'll look at your medical logs and send a copy of the interface data to Jack for analysis. We can run your medical stats alongside the mission recorder from your suit to make sure your physiological reactions are in line with what they should be."

"I trust my team, and they need to trust me. If something is off, we need to address it."

"Absolutely. We'll get to the bottom of it," the doctor assured her. "It could be a product of the new AI interface, or it might be something related to the nanites. Or maybe it's nothing at all."

Kira nodded. "Thank you, Doctor."

Elric examined the results of her body scan. "In the meantime, everything looks normal. Well, your *new* normal. The nanites seem to have settled in."

"How so?"

"They multiplied and embedded in your musculoskeletal system. I believe that must be what's given you the enhanced strength, and it would also explain the pain during your transformations as some of the nanites stream outward to form the defensive exoskin. That close integration explains why they were never 'contagious', since they're fully integrated with you," he explained. "Your first full transformation, you didn't experience the same discomfort because there weren't as many inside you yet. They absorbed your suit and the decking in order to propagate."

Kira couldn't help staring at her hands, searching for any signs of the nanites. "I guess it does make me feel a little better to have some sense of what's happening during the transformations."

"I've often found that to be the case with any medical condition." Elric studied her. "Have there been any signs of other abilities… telekinesis?"

"Stars, no!"

"Well, that was one of the goals of these nanites—to replicate TK abilities."

Kira shook her head. "If Monica succeeded in doing that, I haven't experienced any sign of it yet."

"I had to ask." Doctor Elric motioned her down from the exam bed. "I'll be in touch as soon as I've gone through the logs. Try to get some rest."

Kira smiled as she prepared to go. "Yes, Doctor."

As soon as she had exited Medical, Kira messaged Leon at one of the comm consoles. "Hey! I'm back."

"Already? That was quick."

"Don't sound so excited," she jested.

Leon sighed, giving her a warm smile. "*Of course* I'm glad you're back! How'd it go?"

"I'll tell you when we're together."

"Well, I'm at my lab—should be finished with this task in another half hour or so. Should I message you then, or do you want to come here?" he asked.

"How about—" Kira cut off when she saw an incoming message from Colonel Kaen. "Wait, I think I'm being summoned. I'll get back to you," she told Leon.

"See you soon."

Kira switched over to the other call. "Sir, what can I do for you?"

"Major Sandren has filled me in on what happened in Gaelon, but I'd like to hear it directly from you."

Kira's chest tightened. "Yes, sir."

"We're waiting for you in the conference room by my office."

"I'll be there right away."

Kira was thankful Jasmine left her to her own thoughts for the walk. She already had her talking points in mind for each of the likely scenarios. Aside from being court-martialed for gross negligence, her worst fear was being put on desk duty until her condition was fully understood—if that could ever happen. More likely, only her fitness for command would be questioned, and she would remain in the field as a specialized tool for the Guard to direct as it saw fit. While not ideal, that outcome would still be preferable to the other options.

Trying to visualize a favorable result, Kira strode into the conference room with as much confidence as she could muster. Colonel Kaen and Major Sandren were seated behind the long edge of the table opposite the door.

"Sirs," she greeted.

"Have a seat, Captain." Kaen gestured to the chair nearest the entry.

"Sir, if I could explain—"

"All I want to know is what happened to you while you were trying to leave, in your own words," the colonel interrupted.

The request caught Kira off-guard. *Why didn't he lay into me?*

She cleared her throat. "Well, the walls appeared to disintegrate into a swarm of particles. The nearest analogy I can give is that it looked like a sandstorm—except there was no wind. The particles closed in around us, but they let the three other members of my team through, focusing on me. They stuck together and tried to secure me to the ground. We used kinetic rounds to break the bonds, and I was able to escape. They tried the same thing with the shuttle, but we made it out in time."

Kaen nodded. "By your estimation, could the swarm have

disabled the shuttle?"

"With enough time, maybe. Probably."

"I'll talk with General Lucian about getting authorization for a strike," Kaen stated.

Kira gave him a questioning look in spite of herself. "Sir, the external processor—"

"Your team's activities were interrupted by a hostile alien presence, which attempted to disable you and make it impossible to leave. Is that an incorrect assessment of the field report?" Kaen asked.

"No, sir."

<That narrative favors me, but why?> Kira asked Jasmine privately. <I might have made terrible command decisions today. They shouldn't be overlooking that.>

<There's something bigger going on,> Jasmine replied. <They have new information, but I can't access what it is.>

<That doesn't let me off the hook for what happened.>

Jasmine sighed in her mind. <Why are you so intent on being punished? Some tech got left behind. Far worse things have happened on the watch of the greatest Guard leaders.>

<I...> Kira thought about what was really bothering her. <It's because I still don't trust myself. I'm worried that the Trols are manipulating me and we don't know it.>

<If you can't trust yourself, then trust me.>

<I want to, but—>

<It takes time. I know. But you need to focus on the task at hand. I've seen all your records, and I know what you're capable of. Get ahold of yourself and snap out of this funk. We have an enemy to defeat!>

Kira sat in stunned silence as the AI's words sank in. She hadn't expected the sentiment to come from that source, but it was the stern talking-to she'd been craving. That she *needed*.

She returned her attention to Kaen and Sandren. "Sir, do you have a response planned against the aliens?"

"We haven't made a final decision," Kaen replied. "We've just come into some new information that changes our understanding of the situation."

"May I ask what that information is, sir?"

"It came from Ellen Calleti," Sandren explained.

Kira did a double take. "I knew she'd gone back to Mysar, but why is she still getting herself mixed up in our business?"

"Not like last time," he assured her. "In her efforts to help the Mysarans rebuild their government, she came across some records. Well, rather, she went digging. But we'll excuse her foolhardiness, because she stumbled across a data archive. And the facility bears a striking resemblance to the one on the Gaelon dwarf planet."

Kira folded her arms on the tabletop. "I'd say that doesn't make any sense, but we're pretty far past that at this point."

"I share your sentiments." Sandren flashed a wan smile. "At any rate, we've just dug into the contents of that data archive, and it tells an interesting tale. Reya and her associates have been very busy."

"What were they doing?" Kira asked.

"Mining and manufacturing—more than the Elvar Trinary could possibly consume."

<Gaelon,> Jasmine said in her mind at the same time Kira thought it.

"Is that where the material for the artificial dwarf planet came from?" Kira asked aloud.

"We're waiting on the conclusive results, but the preliminary analysis of the samples you collected points to an affirmative," Sandren confirmed.

"What I found more pressing was Ellen's personal

account," Kaen said. "She spoke with someone whom had worked closely with Reya. That woman indicated that others had relayed information to her about some sort of pit underneath the facility where they obtained the data."

A chill spread through Kira's limbs. "A pit like I saw in Gaelon, where they spoke to me."

Kaen nodded. "That was my thought, as well."

Kira sat in silence for a moment. "Sir, if the beings live down in that pit, that may mean that Reya wasn't the only entity on Mysar."

"I have troops ready to keep the peace, if they try something," Kaen assured her. "But from everything we've seen on Mysar, these beings—the Trols, as I saw you named them—like to manipulate things behind the scenes. I doubt we have concern of a violent uprising."

Kira wasn't sure about that, but it wasn't her immediate concern. "There's still the processor on the Gaelon planet, sir. They could become a serious threat if they have time to adapt that technology."

Kaen nodded. "I'm actively working on a solution to answer that threat. Stand by for further instructions."

—   —   —

Studying his girlfriend like a lab specimen wasn't what Leon had envisioned for his new career in the Guard. Even as his tasks kept pointing him in that direction, he refused to lose sight of the person he was fighting for. She was too important to him to be reduced to microscopic datapoints on a screen.

Unfortunately, Jack had no such personal ties. "This tech is so *weird*," he commented for the third time while reviewing Kira's medical logs on the other side of the lab.

"Unless you have something useful to say, could you try to keep your thoughts to yourself?" Leon requested.

"Oh, come on." Jack swiveled around on his stool. "Aren't you a little curious?"

"To look at your analysis of how nanites have transformed someone I care about against her will, and how she now has a computer intelligence in her brain to keep her from transforming? Yeah, I'm sure it's weird and fascinating how all that tech is interacting, but I'm only interested in what will *help* her," Leon shot back.

Jack spun back around with his hands raised in defense. "Whoa, touched a nerve."

Leon took a steadying breath. That may have been an overreaction, but he didn't care. His team needed to remember that there were people behind the science.

Just as he was getting back to work, an alert from Kira popped up on Leon's workstation. He answered her call. "Hi, finished with the meeting?"

"Yeah. Are you still at your lab?"

"I am."

"On my way." Kira ended the call.

"That was very business-y and matter-of-fact," Jack commented from across the lab.

"Not everyone is as lovey-dovey in public as you and Stacy," Tess told him.

Leon glared over his shoulder at Jack. "You were the one talking about her like a lab specimen."

Tess held up her finger. "A smart, pretty, capable lab specimen with thoughts and feelings, and we care about her well-being very much."

Leon sighed. "Should I expect an ongoing analysis of every interaction I have in all aspects of my life?" he said, hoping to get them to mind their own business.

Instead, Tess shrugged. "Well, we're scientists, and we also don't get a lot of action down here in the lab, so… yeah, that's a safe bet."

I really need my own office. Leon pushed back from his workstation. "Why don't you two head out for the day?" he offered pointedly.

"I'm in the middle of something," Jack replied.

"It's okay if *you* step out, though." Tess looked over her shoulder at Leon. "We'll hold down the fort until you get back."

Admittedly, he could use a break. "I won't be gone long."

"Come on, don't sell yourself short!" Jack called out.

It took Leon a moment to realize what he meant, and he decided to leave without dignifying the remark, confident in the knowledge that was one aspect of his relationship with Kira he didn't need to worry about.

He waited in the hall for Kira to arrive. After two minutes, he saw her round the bend.

"What are you doing out here?" she asked. Her brow was tight with worry, and she had uncharacteristic dark circles under her eyes.

Leon walked forward to meet her halfway and pulled her in for a kiss without saying a word.

She kissed him back, the tension releasing from her shoulders.

"Let's go somewhere we can talk alone," he suggested. "My quarters aren't far."

Kira nodded.

He led the way. "Did something happen out there?"

"A lot of things," she murmured.

Leon looked at her with concern.

"We're all fine," she assured him. "These aliens just have

me on edge."

"I know what you mean."

He hated to see her so stressed. Maybe that was her normal state in the Guard, but something told him this was beyond normal. The Robus situation certainly couldn't be helping matters.

I'm sick of feeling like I can't do anything to make this easier on her. Well, maybe I can't from a medical standpoint, but I can still offer love and support. That is within my control.

Leon grabbed her hand as they walked the final stretch to his quarters. She squeezed his back.

He palmed open his door and motioned her inside.

The room was slightly smaller than Kira's, equipped with a double bed between two end tables, a built-in dresser, and a viewscreen on the wall. A door in the center of the right wall led to a compact washroom. He spent so little time in the space that he didn't need anything more.

As soon as they were inside with the door closed, Kira wrapped her arms around his neck and led him toward the bed as her lips found his.

He eagerly kissed her back, having been days since he'd seen her, and going on two weeks since they'd been intimate—since before the discovery of her transformation.

They were just about to recline on the bed when Kira suddenly pulled back. "Hold on a sec."

"What's wrong?"

Kira got a distant look in her hazel eyes for a moment. "Sorry, I wasn't sure how to handle this with an AI in my head. Jasmine and I had to come to an understanding."

"Oh, I guess that *would be* a little weird, having someone watching," Leon realized.

"Yeah, a mental running commentary about my increased

dopamine levels was, shockingly, not enhancing the mood."
Kira drew him down to her. "But don't worry, she won't
interrupt us again."

Forgetting about the silent observer, Leon set about giving
Kira a reprieve from her worries.

CHAPTER 13

KIRA NESTLED AGAINST Leon's bare chest. "Thank you. I needed that."

He kissed her forehead. "You've been distancing yourself. I told you I would be here to help you through this, and I meant it."

She knew she'd been holding back. As much as she wanted to open up to him, it wasn't that easy.

Her family in the Guard was a support network that had proved itself time and time again. To add someone else into that mix was a scary prospect. If she let herself fall for Leon again—as an adult, with the maturity and understanding that came with that kind of relationship—the balance would shift. Though her existing network wouldn't be any less important, there'd be someone else on equal footing, and she needed to know that leg wouldn't be kicked out from under her.

"I'm sorry I never gave us a chance before," she murmured.

Leon looked down at her. "What do you mean?"

"When I left to join the Guard." Kira stared up at the ceiling. "I got scared that I was going to get trapped in a life—

on a future path—before I really knew myself. So I ran away from everything I thought defined me. My world. My parents. You. By the time I'd wised up enough to realize that I could have talked to you about those concerns like a reasonable person, I figured you'd want nothing to do with me."

"I always wondered if it was something I did," he said.

"No." She shook her head. "You were always there for me when I needed you, and in return I was selfish and only thought of myself."

Leon stroked her shoulder. "Well, we have a chance to start over now."

"We do. And to do it right, I know I need to let you in. But I'm not used to being vulnerable," Kira admitted.

"Companionship can make us stronger. Just look at you with your team."

She looked up at him. She saw the love in his eyes—his unwavering dedication to her, despite everything she'd been through in the last two weeks. If that wasn't enough to scare him off, then nothing would.

"I want you to be a part of my team," she told him. "I mean, be here with me."

Leon shifted to his side to face her. "I love you, Kira."

Her heart melted, just like when she had been a teenager hearing the words for the first time, and then a warm glow filled her. She wasn't that girl anymore, and what was between them now spoke to a deeper bond between the selves they'd grown into over the years.

"I love you, too. I want to see things through this time, the way I wasn't ready to before."

Their lips met again, and Kira lost herself in the moment.

When they eventually parted, neither could keep from grinning.

<Awww!> Jasmine exclaimed in Kira's mind.

<Jasmine!> she mentally scolded.

<Sorry. This is overwhelming for me, too. I'm not used to processing these emotions!>

Kira sighed. "For what it's worth, Jasmine approves," she told Leon.

He chuckled. "Glad to hear I pass muster."

<I'll say,> Jasmine added in Kira's mind. *<Based on how you were feeling a few minutes ago—>*

<Thanks, Jasmine. I've got this.>

Kira blocked out the AI as best she could to return her focus to Leon. "I can't promise to always be the most attentive partner, but I'll be honest and fair with you."

He gave her another kiss. "I can't ask for anything more."

They lay together for a few minutes longer, and then Kira's mind wandered to the unresolved tasks from earlier in the day. "Hey, did you talk with Doctor Elric about the medical data that Jasmine recorded while I was on the op?"

"Aaand the moment is over." Leon sat up.

"Sorry, I'll work on my transitions." She ran her hand down his arm.

"Actually, I was just thinking about it, too." He climbed out of bed and began dressing.

Kira did the same. "And?"

"I'm supposed to stop by Medical this afternoon to go over it with him. You're welcome to come along, if you don't mind us talking about your weird brain right in front of you." He smiled.

She balled up a sock and threw it at him, then promptly realized that she needed it.

Leon deflected the fabric ball, and it landed at the foot of the mattress. "It'll be helpful to have you around to answer questions."

Kira dove across the bed to retrieve the wayward sock. "I can remain objective."

"Good."

<I predict copious opinionated interjections,> Jasmine said in Kira's mind.

Says the AI that does that all the time, Kira thought privately.

She gave a mental smile to the AI. *<I said I can remain objective, not that I necessarily would.>*

<I appreciate the distinction.>

<Well, I'd appreciate you letting me have alone time with my boyfriend without narration.>

<You're still angry about that?>

Kira gave a mental eyeroll at the AI's wounded tone. *<Not angry, just looking to set up some boundaries. I know we share this body, but you're not in a relationship with Leon—I am.>*

Jasmine retreated. *<I understand. It won't happen again.>*

<Jasmine… don't be upset.> Kira reached out to her. *<I don't want to argue. Let's just focus on figuring out what happened on Gaelon, okay?>*

<Yes, Kira. I promise to be more respectful of your private space. I've never been paired with someone who's in love. It got the better of my curiosity.>

<I'm sure I would have had the same temptation.> She caught herself. *<Stars, I don't have a right to judge. I've spent my career rooting around in other people's minds.>*

<But we're partners. Mutual respect.>

<Deal.>

When Kira and Leon were dressed in their shipsuits, they headed to Medical.

Doctor Elric was with a patient when they arrived, and a

nurse showed them to the doctor's office in the back right of the infirmary. The desk was situated in the middle of the room facing the door, and a holodisplay behind it was covered with coded reminders about various patient check-ins. Kira spotted her name at the top of the list.

Kira and Leon seated themselves in the visitor chairs.

"I had gotten used to the check-ups after every op, but with these extra visits, I feel like I'm going to practically be living here," Kira whispered.

"I hope not. I'd miss you overnight."

She gave him a coy smile. "I think it's still a little early to think about moving into shared quarters."

He returned the smile. "I never said anything about that. Just, you know—"

"Oh, Kira, I didn't expect to see you again so soon," Doctor Elric said, entering his office.

"I hope you don't mind me sitting in on your discussion with Leon, Doctor," Kira replied, swiveling around in her chair.

"You are the subject, after all. Of course you can be here." The doctor sat down behind his desk.

"I would have taken a look before coming over here, but I didn't receive your analysis," Leon said.

Doctor Elric made entries on his desktop to bring up a file. "Because I never sent it. There were some components that I felt warranted discussion before we draw any conclusions." He folded his hands on the desktop. "Physiologically, it appears that Jasmine was able to regulate neurochemical reactions to prevent the agitated state that has previously triggered an unwanted Robus transformation. However, there were some brainwave patterns that didn't match up with that regulated state."

Kira half-raised her hand. "I know I'm just supposed to be an observer here, but what kind of variance are we talking about?"

<I told you that you wouldn't be able to keep quiet,> Jasmine ribbed in her mind.

<Yeah, well, you were wondering the same thing.>

"At four points during your time on the dwarf planet," Elric continued, "there was a shift in the brainwave pattern—like it had entered a sympathetic resonance."

"Similar to when Kaen and Jared were subverted?" Leon asked.

Elric shook his head. "No, this wasn't a control signal. It was more like a sync."

Kira frowned. "What does that mean in this context?"

"That's what I'm trying to figure out," the doctor replied. "I was hoping to get a record of the *Raven*'s sensor logs, as well as a copy of the environmental data gathered via your armor's sensors, to get a better picture of what may have been going on."

"I was tapped into the suit," Jasmine interjected over the room's comm system.

"Yes, and that was filtered and combined as part of Kira's experience. I'd like to see how that compares to the raw logs," Elric explained.

"Ah, and in that discrepancy may lie the solution," Jasmine stated.

"Precisely." Elric met Leon's gaze. "The reason I wanted to meet with you, Leon, is I have a hunch that this resonance is related to Kira's TR structure."

"Again, not a neuroscientist," Leon muttered under his breath.

Elric shrugged. "You're as close to an expert as we have on

this tech, all the same. This resonance may be a variation of the remote communications we've observed."

Kira came to attention. "If that theory holds, I bet I know exactly which four times the resonance happened—when I entered the rock formation, when we saw the central nexus thing, when we came to the pit, and when we were trying to escape."

Next to her, Leon's expression turned to horror. "I really have no idea what you just said, but that sounds awful."

"It was a fun day." Kira patted his knee. "I can access the mission records on my account, if you want me to log in."

"Please." Elric motioned to the desktop.

Kira placed her hand on the surface to gain access and then navigated to the appropriate directory containing the logs.

"All right, so," she went to the raw logs from her powered armor, "we entered the rock formation right around here."

Using the combat video recorder as a guide, she cycled through the frames until the view matched her recollection. She played it forward for Leon and the doctor.

"Those rocks are so weird-looking," Leon commented, tilting his head.

"Made of valteron," Kira explained.

Leon crossed his arms. "Huh."

Elric leaned forward to study the details. "Yes, that timestamp does align with the first resonance," he confirmed.

"So far so good." Kira advanced the record. "Now, the next…"

Kira selected the footage from when she approached the monolith in the central cavern with her team.

"Hmm, I'm not seeing a spike," Elric observed.

"No, there *has* to be something here," Kira insisted.

Leon looked at her. "What were you expecting?"

"This chamber," Kira pointed to the image on the desktop, "is also composed of valteron. And there's a *lot* of it. I'd expect this place to be a resonance hotspot."

"Maybe it's not that simple," Leon mused. "Just because a material is present doesn't mean that it has an active connection—there might be other factors."

"That's a valid point," Elric agreed. "Maybe the valteron needs to have a signal running through it, or something of the sort."

"Then why did the rocks on the surface cause such a strong reaction?" Kira asked.

"Well, it's the perimeter of the facility. Perhaps there's a trigger of some sort," Leon suggested.

She tilted her head. "Like a security system?"

"Or proximity alarm," Elric said. "You felt faint when you first stepped inside, yes?"

Kira nodded.

"I had to make some significant adjustments to compensate," Jasmine chimed in.

"Not everyone would have an AI capable of cancelling out the effects," Elric continued. "I can only speculate, but the information I've seen points to a net, designed to catch anyone with remotely compatible tech that would enable potential telepathic control."

Kira decided to go with the line of reasoning. "And since I made it out of the net, and my team wasn't susceptible, we were able to proceed. But that's a really ineffective security system, if anyone else can just walk inside."

"Except you didn't find anything," the doctor stated.

"We accessed the computer system and were loading a ton of data onto an external drive," Kira pointed out.

"Yes, but you never got that off the planet. After the

mission, you were essentially in the same place you began," he countered.

"Are you suggesting that it *allowed* us through the facility?"

Elric shrugged. "I don't have enough information to say. Let's go through the rest of the mission recording to see if any patterns emerge."

"Right." Kira continued advancing the video.

"The next spike to your vitals came about ten minutes later," Elric said, consulting his notes.

"Yes, I know exactly what that one was about." Kira braced for the viewing of the next segment—their visit to the mysterious pit.

The voices wouldn't come through on the recording, since Jasmine hadn't heard them, but Kira remembered the chill that had run through her as they'd whispered in her mind.

She resumed playing the video at normal speed at the appropriate point. When the video showed Kira's perspective of looking into the pit, Elric and Leon inched back in their chairs.

"How deep is that?" Leon asked.

"Too deep," Kira replied, knowing her team on the video was about to state the results of the scan. She waited for the onscreen discussion to conclude.

"All right, this is when I heard them," Kira said. She watched Elric follow along with her vitals feed.

"Yes, that's definitely the second resonance spike," the doctor confirmed.

Kira frowned. "That's all well and good, but you said there were four instances of vital spikes. One of the four incidents I had in mind didn't pan out."

Elric nodded. "Based on the end time of the mission record, I can confirm that the last incident corresponds with the attack while you were exiting. The third was approximately six minutes before that, but it wasn't a spike so much as a sustained, low-level increase." He pointed to a timestamp in his notes.

"We were just walking through the hallways. Nothing stands out." Kira skipped ahead to the timestamp the doctor had indicated.

When she reached the point in the recording, the doctor's observation suddenly made sense. "Of course, that's when we entered the exit tunnel."

"They may have been subtly influencing you, trying to get you to stay," Elric suggested.

"I didn't feel it at all." Up until that point, Kira had been confident that she'd know if she was under the aliens' influence. Now, she wasn't so sure.

<Did you notice anything, Jasmine?> she asked her AI privately.

<I thought it had something to do with your nanites, so I was trying to keep you balanced. I know what to look for in the future and what it may mean.>

<Lesson learned all around.>

Kira looked between Leon and Doctor Elric. "We know the circumstances around the telepathic resonance now, but why was it just those four times? Was it a communication attempt and I missed it?"

"It's strange that nothing happened in the main chamber, like you said," Leon replied. "If they were trying to communicate, I'd think they'd do it in the place with the most valteron to act as a conduit."

"I agree. The fact that nothing happened in that chamber is an anomaly," Elric said.

Leon's eyes narrowed in thought. "These guys are smart.

All of their moves have been calculated and intentional."

"That's what worries me." Kira slumped in her seat. "I can't shake the feeling that we were the ones being investigated, not the other way around."

"Or hunted," Leon said. He straightened in his chair and had a spark in his eyes.

"Yeah, that makes me feel *way* better." She shot him a venomous look.

Leon shook his head. "I didn't mean it facetiously. I've been trying to think through the behavior from a biological standpoint—analyze it in terms of the traits we know to be evolutionarily beneficial. I think I have a working theory."

"These things are unlike anything else we've seen," Kira reminded him.

"But in broad strokes, there are predators and prey," Leon began. "On the prey side, when a threat is spotted, creatures either run or freeze, with the hope they aren't spotted."

"But the alien-particle-things attacked us while we were trying to leave," Kira countered.

"That's what got me thinking," Leon continued. "We can't see these beings, so it's easy for them to hide. But it doesn't follow the prey pattern of waiting for a threat to pass and then coming out of hiding. They're hunters. They set a trap for what they wanted, and when it didn't work, they waited for another opportunity to strike."

Kira crossed her arms and sighed. "I knew that whole thing was a trap."

"But how, specifically?" Doctor Elric prompted. "Why not go after the team when they were deepest inside the facility?"

"That's the part that didn't click for me until just now," Leon went on. "Like any predator, they have their preferred hunting grounds. In this case, they lured you, Kira—the prey—

toward their hiding place. The first trap didn't work, and they also saw that you had backup. So, they waited for you to go to another location where they knew they could corner you." He pointed to the video again. "You were behind everyone else. It's the only point in your entire walk through the facility that the rest of the team was closer to an exit than you were."

"Shite, you're right!" she realized. "I had consistently been walking in between them except for that moment."

"And that's when they tried to snare you in a different sort of trap—a stronger, better one."

Her stomach turned over. "And it almost worked."

Elric nodded. "They don't have a good understanding of our technology, despite their apparent integration into Mysaran society. But, the Mysarans also don't have Empire tech."

"Okay, so we were able to catch them by surprise with firepower superior to what they were anticipating, and we got free," Kira said. "But none of this answers why they wanted me, and only me, in the first place. Wouldn't it be worthwhile to take the rest of my team, too?"

"Not if they're purely after *you*—or the physiological model of how your nanites have changed you, a native Valtan," Leon replied. "I haven't done a lot of fighting, but I do know it's better to get an opponent on their own. The more soldiers the Trols captured, the harder it would be for them to contain you."

Kira crossed her arms and leaned back. "That's a riveting analysis and all, but it tells us nothing we didn't already know. This only confirms our suspicions that they're on the offensive."

She realized that Doctor Elric had disengaged from the conversation and was looking over data logs on the desktop.

He met her gaze with a slack jaw. "There's something we missed."

"I took the liberty of going through the *Raven*'s sensor logs while you were talking, to compare the resonance readings and activity timeline with what was going on elsewhere on the world," Jasmine said over the comm.

"And there was definitely something." Elric zoomed in on what he had been examining.

A line indicating the ambient readings around the planet was relatively smooth for hours, and then rhythmic spikes initiated at the timestamp when Kira and her team exited the stairwell. The intensity of the spikes increased during the time they were in the central chamber and then dropped off again.

Leon frowned. "What is that?"

"I don't know, exactly," Elric admitted.

Kira did. She'd been on enough ops and used enough communication systems to recognize those patterns anywhere.

"It's a transmission," she stated. "The *valley* around the facility wasn't the transmitter—it's the whole planet."

CHAPTER 14

EVEN WITH THE Guard working on an analysis of the data retrieved from the valley lab, Ellen found her thoughts drifting back to the facility and what she'd seen.

I can't begin rebuilding this world so long as I know there's something lurking down there. She slumped in her desk chair. If that 'something' was what she feared it was, no one would be safe.

When Kira and her team had come to the Mysaran government building and subdued Chancellor Hale, Ellen had wondered about how the alien could go down so easily. A race capable of projecting their consciousness across systems wouldn't give up on a three-decades-long mission because one host was gone.

Ellen had trusted the Guard when they said they'd eliminate the threat, but they were focused on Gaelon. There was a facility only kilometers from the city where Ellen presently resided, and it was too connected to the aliens for her liking.

Naturally, the Guard hadn't shared a bomaxed thing about

what they'd learned in their investigations. Fortunately, Ellen had her own sources.

She walked down the short hall to Fiona's office. The other woman finished up a call and then beckoned her inside.

"Hi, I wanted to ask you about those people you used to send to the facility in the valley," Ellen said.

Fiona's brow knitted. "I thought you handed that matter over to the Guard?"

"They're focused on Gaelon. I want to know if we have a threat *here*."

"That can wait for the Guard to look into."

"How can you be so sure we're not in danger *right now*?"

"I'm not," Fiona admitted. "But this isn't something we can handle. It's dangerous to look too deep."

"Do you have any other leads or sources?" Ellen fixed her with a level gaze, sensing that Fiona was holding back.

"There's a man," Fiona said reluctantly. "He's the only person I know of who spent time in that facility. However, he's never said more than five words about it."

"I'd like to speak with him," Ellen requested. "I can't focus on vetting political candidates until I'm confident that another subverted person can't worm their way in."

"Keep talking like that, and you're going to find yourself in charge," Fiona said.

Right! That would be the day. Ellen dismissed the notion. "Can you set up a meeting?"

"An appointment isn't necessary. He lives in a care facility."

Ellen frowned. "Oh."

Fiona looked down at her hands. "He was never quite right after the assignment. I'm not proud of my part in what happened to the people on this world."

Ellen was touched by the remorse in her tone. "That's all the more reason for us to make sure no one else can get hurt. If there's *any* chance these aliens are still here on Mysar, we need to be prepared."

"I don't know if Edgar can tell you anything useful, but I'll take you to see him," Fiona agreed.

They headed to the train station and boarded the main line connecting the domes.

Fiona took a seat away from the door. "We're headed to Dome 5."

"Ah, I should have guessed." Ellen settled in for a long ride.

The domes hadn't been planned to have any distinction among social strata, but like any society, people had sorted themselves into classes. Dome 1 was fair game for anyone to visit, being the commercial center, but only the wealthiest could afford apartments in the high-rise towers overlooking the parks. The other domes were ranked in preference roughly according to their numeric value. That put Dome 5 at the bottom.

Ellen had spent most of her previous time on Mysar in Dome 3, which housed the university where she and Leon had attended school. Once she began working for the government, she'd found a small apartment at a reasonable rent rate and commuted to the remote capitol building for work. In her years living there, she'd made a point of avoiding Dome 5.

While not dangerous or dirty, per se, it attracted the kind of people who didn't want to integrate with the rest of society in a productive way. With drugs being an issue for some members of the district's population, the hospital offered a necessary service—more of a clinic, really, compared to the main medical center in Dome 1.

Anyone with ongoing issues would be admitted as a

resident in the clinic, which made for the perfect place to hide a witness. No one took the ramblings of former drug addicts and their associates seriously.

Ellen stared out the window as the train wove around the outskirts of Dome 1 and into the tunnel connected to Dome 5. As she anticipated, there was a distinct shift in the train's passengers the closer they got to their destination.

They got off at the fourth stop after the tunnel.

"Do you come here often?" Ellen asked as they left the platform.

"I've only visited him twice," Fiona replied, looking straight ahead. "That was enough."

Fiona's path took them five blocks to the west, past modest shops and restaurants that would have been considered a hole-in-the-wall in other districts.

The destination was a five-story concrete building with slit windows. To Ellen's eye, it looked more like a prison than a medical clinic.

Maybe it is.

They checked in at a reception desk inside the front door, and a nurse wearing white scrubs came out to meet them.

"Edgar hasn't had any visitors for a while. Are you friends of his?" the middle-aged woman asked.

"Yes, from back in school," Fiona replied.

Ellen permitted the lie, not wanting to raise unwanted questions.

"I'll take you to him." The nurse led them to an elevator, which they took to the third floor.

The elevator opened into a lobby with a security gate around the perimeter.

Ellen's skin crawled. *This is definitely not a place where people voluntarily reside.*

Through the gate, a short hallway was lined with numbered doors, which eventually opened into a common room filled with seating and entertainment screens. Half a dozen patients were situated around the room, most absorbed in their own activities.

"There he is," the nurse said, pointing to a man in his late-thirties.

Ellen and Fiona thanked the nurse and approached him.

Edgar was seated by one of the narrow windows, rocking back and forth in his chair. One hand was formed into a fist pressed over his mouth. Dark circles ringed his blood-shot eyes, as though he hadn't had a proper night's sleep in months.

"What happened to him?" Ellen whispered.

"We've never been able to get a full story," Fiona replied. "As part of my responsibilities, I was tasked with getting him set up in a place where people wouldn't ask too many questions. It's such a small world, we didn't have many options outside this hospital."

Ellen watched the man continue to rock. "Will he talk to me?" she asked Fiona.

"You can try."

Ellen grabbed a chair from an unoccupied table nearby and stepped up to Edgar. "Hi, Edgar, my name is Ellen. Do you mind if I sit with you?"

His gazed darted to her briefly, but he made no other indication.

She decided to take it that he didn't oppose and sat down across from him. "I'm here as a government consultant. I heard you spent some time at a facility in a valley outside the city."

Edgar stopped rocking and removed his hand from over his mouth. His eyes grew so wide that she could see the whites almost all the way around. "Don't ever go there. It's *evil*."

"I don't want to, but I'm worried that the badness there might try to get out."

"No, they stay in the pit." He took a series of sharp, rapid breaths. "They always stay in the pit."

"Did you ever see them?"

He brought his knees up to his chest with his feet resting on the seat of the chair, arms wrapped around his shins. "The whispers. So many voices."

"Anything more you can tell me would help," Ellen pressed. She felt for the man, but cryptic answers didn't get her what she needed.

Edgar began rocking again. "We'll take them—take them all. They'll bleed and suffer. Pain. They'll long for death that won't come. We'll feed. First Elusia and then the rest."

Ellen's heart skipped a beat. "Is that what the voices said?"

The man made no response, but tears formed in his eyes. He took a shaky breath and released it as a whimper.

"I doubt he'll say any more," Fiona said. "You can't reach him once he's like this."

Ellen rose and put the chair back where she found it. "I need to talk with President Joris."

— — —

Kira and Leon huddled around the holodisplay in one of the small briefing rooms. Doctor Elric had been a good sport while they theorized the aliens' motivations, but the medical doctor needed to attend to his patients.

At Jasmine's suggestion, Kira and Leon had adjourned to finish their discussion while the ideas were still fresh. Once they had their thoughts organized, they could bring a working hypothesis to Sandren and Kaen.

Getting to that point, however, was proving difficult.

"A planet-sized thing can't possibly be for the purpose of controlling one person," Kira insisted.

Leon blinked slowly and took a deep breath. "That's not what I'm saying at all. All I meant is that the signal must be able to differentiate recipients. Even if there only happens to be one receiver at a given moment, the whole structure will still activate. How many simultaneous signals it can send out is a huge unknown."

"How do we determine where the signal is going?" Kira asked. "Can we trace it, like we did with Jared?"

"We can run a search for that specific signal and radiation signatures we've associated with the Trols," Jasmine said over the room's comm for Leon's benefit. "I can look through the logs to see if it pops up anywhere else."

"Do it," Kira told her.

"I don't like any of this," Leon muttered.

Kira crossed her arms. "Me either."

"You're going to like this even less," Jasmine said after a minute.

"You have a hit already?" Kira asked.

"Didn't have to look far. The gas giant on the other side of the sun emitted a resonant signal two point seven seconds after the planet broadcast."

"What does it mean for us?" Kira asked. "Is there something receiving the signal on the planet?"

Leon tilted his head. "Oh… that's intriguing."

"Hmm?" Nothing on the screen jumped out at her.

"The resonant signal from the gas giant is stronger than the one sent from the artificial planet."

"I believe it's a bio-amplifier," Jasmine jumped in. "A signal booster, if you will. Upon re-analysis of the *Raven*'s scans in the system, I have detected that the gas giant emits an echo of signals bouncing around the system. Its atmosphere appears to contain trace amounts of valteron. The scans indicate that it exists in an organism that feeds on hydrogen and methane."

Kira scratched her head. "My biology is really fuzzy."

Leon shrugged.

"Such an organism would be self-replicating," Jasmine continued. "Over time, sending a signal of the same strength would produce a stronger and stronger resonance effect. If the dwarf planet is indeed a transmitter, the gas giant is a self-sustaining megaphone with ever-increasing volume."

Kira scowled. "I don't like the sound of that. Who are they talking to?"

"Or is it *for* them?" Leon countered. "We know they project themselves over great distances to exert telepathic control."

"Could this be what allowed them to link to Kaen and Jared, all the way to Guard headquarters?" Kira wondered aloud.

"Perhaps," the AI confirmed. "Linking the signal to biological resonance for those with innate telepathic abilities would maximize the likelihood of success."

Kira paused. "Wait, say that again."

"Linking the—"

"No, rephrase it another way," Kira instructed.

"One method to improve communication is by tapping into naturally occurring extrasensory abilities," Jasmine said.

"Telepathy and biological resonance," Kira mused. "That sounds an awful lot like Valta."

Leon's eyes widened. "Yeah, it does."

"If the trace amounts in the gas giant are enough to

produce this magnified effect, then using Valta in the same way would produce exponential results," Jasmine concluded.

Kira's pulse spiked. "We need to find out if there are any other worlds like this."

"I'll get authorization from Colonel Kaen to arrange a scan around the neighboring systems," Jasmine confirmed.

Leon took a slow breath. "It might not be nearby."

That was an unfavorable possibility Kira couldn't ignore. "Question is, what would they want to control from a distance?"

— — —

Kaen sighed. *I can't wait to go back to the enemies with ships and bodies that we can shoot, like civilized soldiers.*

He was about to read some recent mission briefs to distract himself from the Trols when his desktop illuminated with an incoming call from Elusia.

Joris is persistent, I'll give him that.

"President Joris, what can I do for you?" Kaen greeted, plastering on a smile.

"Colonel, thank you for taking my call. I know you have many more pressing issues than Elusia. However, I was hoping to get an update on where your investigation stands regarding Gaelon?"

I've never told him that's where we're investigating. Kaen's eyes narrowed. "Why do you ask about that system?"

"Ellen has uncovered some information regarding Hale's former activities, which point there. I have a hunch your leads indicated the same system."

No sense denying it now. Kaen nodded. "We completed an evaluation and are in the process of determining the best way to eliminate the threat."

"May I ask what you found?" Joris pressed.

"The details are classified," Kaen replied. "Given that your world is involved in this matter by proximity, I appreciate your concerns. I assure you, we'll relay any critical information once we have a full understanding of the situation."

The president frowned. "If I may be candid, I recognize that this is a military matter. But as a member of the Empire, the Guard *is* our military, and I need to be aware of any threat to my people."

World leaders have a way of trying to make themselves the center of the universe.

Kaen took a calming breath. "To be equally candid, we're still gathering information. Unless you have something new to add to that investigation, I respectfully request that you let me do my job."

"Ellen was able to find someone who'd been inside a facility on Mysar with a strange pit."

Kaen came to attention. "What about it?"

"They heard the voices," Joris said. "I think you'll be interested in what those voices had to say."

CHAPTER 15

FOLLOWING THEIR BRAINSTORMING session, Kira and Leon took the opportunity to get in a workout. While not quite as much fun as the exercise earlier in the day, it was nice to be able to fall back into a routine that didn't involve a quarantine chamber and shackles.

Kira set down the weights after their third set. Next to her, Leon was flushed and sweating.

"I could keep up with you before, but it's not fair with your new upgrades," he said through panting breaths.

"You don't need to match me move for move," she replied.

He stretched his arms and legs. "I have to push myself if I want to improve."

"And here you were worried about not being tough enough for the Guard." She smiled.

They completed one more set and then headed to their respective quarters to shower.

As she was stepping out of the shower in her washroom, Kira's comm chirped with an incoming message. She wrapped a towel around herself and answered it, voice only.

"We have new information from Ellen Calleti," Sandren stated. "She made a discovery on Mysar that connects to our ongoing investigation."

"What kind of discovery, sir?"

"We'll discuss at 16:00. Leon and the colonel will meet us in the standard briefing room."

Kira checked the clock; that was in ten minutes. "Yes, sir. On my way."

She quickly dressed and then sent Leon a message for them to meet up at the end of his residential hall, which was on the way from her location.

He was waiting for her when she arrived. "Ellen really knows how to insert herself into the middle of things, doesn't she?" Kira commented. "Not to mention, that woman can't keep her mouth shut."

"Ugh, I know." Leon sighed. "Did Sandren say any more about the new information she discovered?"

"Just that she found something on Mysar that connected to our findings in Gaelon," Kira replied while they headed for the briefing room. "If Kaen and Sandren have called a meeting with us, it must be significant."

"Finally putting together a plan of action?" Leon questioned.

"Let's hope so."

They arrived at the conference room and found that Sandren and Kaen hadn't yet arrived. Kira and Leon took seats by the door and waited for the two officers.

"It's frustrating having most of the image but to still be missing key pieces of the plan," Leon muttered. "Some of the motivation, some of the means, but it doesn't connect."

"As one of those pieces, I can assure you it's much more unsettling from where I'm sitting."

He reached over and took her hand. "Sorry."

Kira quickly extracted her hand when Kaen and Sandren entered.

"It's about time we take over this conference room and stick up a theory board with lines connecting all the dots, eh?" Sandren jested.

"Does that mean Ellen didn't offer up a unifying theory of everything?" questioned Kira.

"Not yet, but we did get another clue," Kaen replied. "Since her debrief following the incident with Chancellor Hale, it would seem Ellen has been on the lookout for suspicious activity. Today she discovered evidence of a pit on Mysar, which sounds suspiciously like the one you found on the planet in Gaelon."

Kira frowned. "Oh, that sounds bad."

"It is," Kaen said with a heavy sigh that concerned Kira more than his words. "We just got the results of the scans for that signal. Aside from the gas giant, it's also somehow resonating with Mysar and Valta."

Kira and Leon exchanged glances.

"What was the timing?" Kira asked.

"Too fast to be through normal space. There must be a subspace component," Sandren responded.

"Hmm." Leon placed his hand on his chin.

Kaen gave him a quizzical look. "Idea?"

"Sorry, it's tangential to this. One of the mysteries has been about the nanites' replication. If this nanotech has some sort of subspace connection, that might explain how the nanites are able to draw enough energy to quickly transmute matter while also venting heat and radiation from the conversion process."

"I guess that does make sense, in a way," Sandren said. "The long-range telepathic control seems to operate like a subspace comm link."

"Which makes the dwarf planet a... giant subspace signal transmitter? But for *what*??" Kira looked at the faces around the table.

"I suggest we go back to what we learned about Monica's research on Valta," Leon suggested. "They were trying to make soldiers."

"And I was supposed to be the template for that," Kira said.

"Right. Breaking that template down to its components," he gave her an apologetic grimace, "there's a telepathic receptor, enhanced physical strength and veracity, and super-speed."

"All things one would hope to have in a soldier," Kaen stated. "Well, except maybe the telepathic part."

"That's the key," Leon said, shaking his index finger. "They wanted a soldier they could control. And control remotely."

Kira folded her hands on the tabletop. "That's an interesting point. Is the degree of control based on length of time paired with a host or distance from the transmitter?"

He nodded. "Exactly. Now, Colonel Kaen, Nox was with you for three years. Even after that much time, you were still able to exert enough control to overpower the being for short bursts."

"Yes," he acknowledged. "But perhaps it didn't fully integrate with me in order to avoid raising flags in my medical exams."

"You modified your own records, yes?" Leon questioned.

"I did, but those were subtle clues. It would have been a different matter if real-time scans found something anomalous."

"Hmm." Leon crossed his arms. "Maybe it's nothing, then."

"No, go on," Sandren encouraged.

"Well," Leon continued, "I was going to contrast Hale's condition to Kaen's. Reya had complete control of her, and Gaelon is a lot closer to Mysar than it is to Orion Station."

An icy vise gripped Kira's chest. "The control point may be even closer than that," she murmured.

"What are you thinking?" Kaen prompted.

"That pit on Mysar. What if those pits are their nests, or whatever you want to call it?"

Sandren paled. "If that's the case, when Hale died, the being never left Mysar."

Kira nodded. "Reya may never have been based in Gaelon, like Nox was."

Kaen swore under his breath. "How many more of these nests could there be?"

"No way to know, sir." Kira replied. "But if the other planets resonated with the signal from Gaelon, that might give us some indication."

"Running a broad scan like that would take weeks, or longer," Sandren said.

"Could we put the locations of the planets up on a map?" Leon spoke up.

"Why?" Kira asked.

"If they have nests in Gaelon *and* Mysar, they don't need a long-range transmitter to communicate in those systems. So, where else were they planning to send their soldiers?"

Without commentary, Sandren hurriedly brought up a holographic map and plotted the real-time location of the four worlds in question.

Everyone stared at the resulting image in stunned silence. The artificial dwarf planet and gas giant in Gaelon were nearly in line on opposite sides of the system's star. That line continued through Mysar and the Elvar star, and ended with Valta. The configuration was mere days from coming into full alignment.

"That's not a coincidence," Kira whispered.

"No, I'd wager it's not." Kaen manipulated the model and zoomed it out so he could extend the line beyond the two systems. Once complete with Valta, it would be headed straight for the worlds in the core of the Taran Empire.

The aliens' motivations were clear. Kira swore under her breath. "They were never just trying to get the Mysaran military to go after Elusia. They were just waiting to make their big move."

"Like a parasite," Leon murmured. "Using up its host and then moving on to the next, to continue to multiply."

"Are they only after the raw elemental materials? Or the people to make more soldiers?" Sandren cut in. "What're they specifically after—what's the end game?"

"Suffering," Kaen said with a grunt. "They feed on negative emotions. The first step was to cultivate a food source—the disgruntled population of Mysar. It sustained them while they put the next phase in action: creating a militia to be their reapers. Peaceful Elusia was the perfect target destination to send their new soldiers, where they could rain down suffering on the innocents."

Leon looked like he was about to be sick. "They made all those preparations without us knowing."

"They could go after Elusia with just anyone—they already had subverted Mysaran soldiers," Sandren said.

Kaen nodded. "But those soldiers couldn't accomplish their ultimate ends of expansion. Elusia would just be a snack to fuel them for the real objective."

Sandren's expression turned grim. "Other Empire worlds."

"Except, following Leon's hypothesis, it appears that their telepathic influence weakens when it gets too far away," Kaen continued. "But with a more robust physical form and enhanced telepathic links, the Robus soldiers they sought to create using Kira as a template would likely be effective at longer distances. Having such a soldier as a vessel, the Trols could roam the galaxy to feed on the suffering they inflicted without breaking their connection to their safe base in Gaelon."

The meeting attendees sat quietly as they processed the realization. Even if some of the details were off, the facts fit too well to dismiss the hypothesis entirely.

"If they weren't so evil, I'd be impressed with the ingenuity," Kira broke the silence.

"A planet-sized bio-amplifier is pretty brilliant," Leon agreed.

"Evilness and aptitude aren't up for debate here. The question remains: how do we stop them?" Kaen looked around the table.

"The way I see it, sir," Kira replied, "their plans hinge on the dwarf planet in Gaelon. We destroy that transmitter and it'll cripple them."

Sandren nodded. "We need to address that immediate known threat. If Gaelon is a home base, which it seems to be, the best action is to cut off the head of the beast."

"Agreed." Kaen nodded. "Based on what we know, any suggestions for the best approach to take these Trols out?"

"Aside from a big boom?" Kira asked.

"I'm not sure we could trust conventional weapons for a task like this," Kaen said. "Completely annihilating a planet is a tall order, even for a fleet."

Kira sat up straight. "It's been done with a single ship,

during the Bakzen War."

Kaen frowned. "That would require calling in the TSS. I'm not even sure if that ship is still in commission."

The *Conquest* was famous even outside the annals of the TSS. The ship was fitted with an ateron relay system, specifically designed to focus telekinetic energy. Few TSS Agents had the raw power to operate the weapon, but it could be turned into a planet-killer in the right hands.

"It may be worth considering, sir," Sandren said. "I know the TSS has started to demilitarize, but a weapon like that would be much more... thorough than anything the Guard could throw at the planet."

"If I may interject," Jasmine said over the comm.

Kaen nodded.

"The *Conquest*'s TK weapon would be effective in the Gaelon System, but addressing the other Trol 'pits', such as on Mysar, will require a more targeted approach, due to the nearby populations," the AI said.

"We can pick off the survivors afterward," Kaen replied.

"I advise against that approach," Jasmine stated.

Kaen tilted his head. "Why is that?"

"Because we don't know how these beings move, or exist, or... anything, really. As a scientist, I must err on the side of caution. Remove the option for the enemy to retreat before you engage."

"You mean, take out the pit on Mysar first?" Kira clarified.

"Yes. There may be other strongholds, but if we don't know about them, that suggests they aren't an immediate threat. Mysar *is*. Make sure those people are safe, and then blow up that Gaelon planet."

<Jasmine, I'm surprised to hear this side of you!> Kira said privately to the AI.

<I think you're rubbing off on me.>

"I'll take it under advisement," Kaen acknowledged. "Now, if you'll excuse me, I have some calls to make."

CHAPTER 16

KIRA FOUND HER team working out in the gym. The three soldiers were in the middle of a wrestling match, so Kira allowed them to settle the competition before she announced herself.

Not surprisingly, Ari came out on top.

"Well done!" Kira called out.

"Kira? When did you get here?" Kyle asked.

"Only a few minutes ago," she replied while walking over.

Nia gestured to the mat. "Care to join us?"

"Not now. I came to fill you in on what's going on with Gaelon."

The members of her team came to attention.

"I wish it was better news," Kira continued. "We've just learned that the Trols have harnessed a bio-amplifier to boost their telepathic signals."

"Should we know what that means?" Nia asked, looking around the circle.

"Details aren't necessary. The point is, that signal strength is about to get a whole lot stronger, and we suspect that the aliens have something planned."

Ari crossed his arms. "What's the plan?"

"Kaen is trying to get access to the TSS *Conquest*." Kira smiled in spite of herself. It wasn't every day they got to witness such powerful technology. Not that she had much hope of being able to actually see it in action, but getting to watch the footage from the ship's records would still be an experience.

"Holy shite." Kyle whistled.

Ari shrugged. "While seeing a TK weapon in action would be spectacular, I wouldn't mind getting my hands dirty."

"Too many firefights in the last two weeks have made you bloodthirsty," Nia ribbed.

"We *have* seen a lot of action. I thought we were back to covert ops, and then this whole mess happened." Kira sighed. "Not to mention everything with me."

"Yeah, how are you doing with your... condition?" Nia asked her.

"It seems to be going well now," Kira replied. "I mean, well enough. Nothing unexpected has happened since my pairing with Jasmine."

"You two still getting along?" Nia looked up while asking the question, indicating that Jasmine was included in the question.

"I am quite pleased with our pairing," Jasmine replied over the comm. "Kira has introduced me to many new experiences."

<*Don't you dare say a word about me and Leon,*> Kira warned in her mind.

<*Don't they know you two are together?*>

<*Yes, but it's different when it's explicit.*>

<*Is there really that big of a distinction?*> Jasmine questioned.

<*There's a lot of subtlety to our lives, I'll leave it at that,*>

Kira told her. <*Ari doesn't need any more fuel.*>

Jasmine smiled in her mind. <*Soon you'll get even.*>

Kira returned her attention to her team. "Jasmine and I are working well together."

Unfortunately, Jasmine's statement hadn't been lost on Ari. "That was a deflection. What aren't you saying?"

Kira decided the best distraction from her new relationship status was to get back to the bad guys. Talk about evil telepathic aliens never got old.

"Before our pairing, Jasmine worked almost entirely in medical labs. We didn't want to freak you out with the idea of having someone along with no combat experience."

"You're the one holding the weapons," Ari pointed out.

Good, he took the bait. Kira nodded. "Yes, but in this particular matter, she's helping to regulate my physiology so I don't transform without meaning to. Some degree of a neurochemical surge is necessary in our line of work—Jasmine is still learning how much is useful to me. We think, back on the Gaelon planet, she may have dialed it back too much for me, and that's why I wasn't feeling anxious when it seemed like I should have been."

Nia eyed her. "Yeah, you were acting off."

<*Or it was the aliens trying to get you to stay,*> Jasmine interjected in Kira's mind.

<*No need to make them worry about that.*>

<*I thought you wanted to be open and honest with them about everything related to missions?*>

Kira sighed. She *was* trying to hide the truth, probably because she didn't want to admit to herself how close she'd come to succumbing to their trap.

"There's something else we discovered," she went on. "When the dwarf planet was sending out those telepathic frequency bursts, it was interacting with me. While we were going down that exit tunnel, I may have been under a subtle telepathic influence."

Kyle's brow furrowed. "So, they *can* get to you."

"I'm not sure," Kira replied. "It wasn't complete. I think it may have been something to do with the proximity to the pit, which seems to be a kind of nest for them. A source of strength and power."

"Hmm," Ari mused. "And their control weakens the further away they are, like when Kaen was way out here?"

"Exactly." Kira nodded. "For all we know, it's possible that all of us were being influenced in some small way while on the Gaelon planet. This isn't an enemy we can predict or understand with what little we know about them."

"All the more reason to blow up the planet and be done with it," Ari muttered.

"We may still have an issue on Mysar," Kira continued. "It appears that there's a pit on that world, too, and that may be where more of the beings live."

Nia's mouth dropped open. "And you didn't lead with that?"

"What's the plan to deal with *that* situation?" Kyle asked at the same time.

"It's a work in progress," Kira replied.

"Hold on," Nia said. "That means Reya was close to a pit when you overpowered her."

"I guess she was," Kira realized. She'd been so preoccupied with thinking about how Reya may have escaped Chancellor Hale when the body died that she'd missed the other implications. "Maybe I *can* stand up to them."

"We always knew that, Kira," Kyle said with a smile. "Don't sound so surprised."

"After what happened on Gaelon, I was having serious doubts," she admitted.

"Fortunately, you have us to believe in you," Ari said.

Kira smiled at her team. "I don't know what I'd do without you guys."

Ari tapped his chin. "I'm torn between you either wasting your gifts as a carnival-style fortune teller or going dark after pushing away everything you ever loved and becoming a super villain."

Kira stared at him. "Wow, you have a very high opinion of the moderating effect of your friendship."

"We *are* pretty awesome," Kyle added.

"For what it's worth, I think you'd only use your super villain powers to go after other bad guys," Nia said, patting Kira on the arm.

"Thanks, I think?" Kira gave the group a quizzical look. "Anyway, since I *am* a Guard officer, and not those strange alternate reality versions of me, we'll be working within the official channels to take care of the Trols."

"Which means… more waiting?" Nia asked.

"For now, but not much longer," Kira told them. "We have a constrained timeline, so I expect we'll be heading out within the day."

Ari's eyed narrowed. "Constrained by *what*?"

"Less than four days until the planets are aligned," Kira muttered.

Kyle exchanged glances with the others. "Wait, planetary alignment? With the bio-amplifier."

Kira gave him a reassuring smile she didn't quite believe in. "Nothing to worry about."

He frowned. "Isn't that kind of a poor design, needing planets to align? It's incredibly rare for everything to sync up."

"I mean, it's planets we're talking about here, so the scale for what you'd consider a straight line is a little arbitrary. The timeline is fuzz," Kira said. "Point is, we want to act before the Trols do."

Her team still looked uneasy, but they nodded.

"Take care of any business around here that you need to," she advised. "We may be deploying on short notice."

"Aye," they acknowledged in unison.

"I'll be in touch as soon as I have instructions." She gave them a parting nod and headed into the hallway.

<How do you decide which information to share with your team?> Jasmine asked once they were alone.

<I trust my instincts,> Kira replied. *<Tell them enough to be motivated, but not so much that it's overwhelming.>*

<Ah, intuition. I am still learning to appreciate the nuances.>

<You're young like me,> Kira said. *<The more we experience, the better our gut instincts will be.>*

Her stomach rumbled.

<Jasmine, was that you?> Kira asked.

<Sorry, I couldn't resist.>

Kira rolled her eyes. *<Oh, hey, speaking of messing with physiology, did Jack ever post any findings about my nanites after he reviewed your field recordings?>*

<He did,> Jasmine replied. *<The report begins: 'The behavior of Kira's nanites is weird.'>*

<Seriously? That's the actual opening line of the official report?>

<It is.>

Suddenly, Kira had a better appreciation for what Leon contended with in the lab on a daily basis.

<Does the report go on to say anything useful?> she

questioned the AI.

<It confirms what we already suspected. The nanites trigger a transformation with relatively low biochemical shifts in your physiology. In other words, you could sustain the state for an extended time.>

<That does fit with the theory that these soldiers were designed to torture victims to prolong the negative experience.>

<Yes,> Jasmine agreed. *<But the 'weirdness' part of the report is in relation to something that we had missed when we were looking only at the higher-level expression. When you were on Gaelon, on the verge of transforming, the signs of what I now know to be subtle telepathic influence were diminished.>*

The revelation caught Kira by surprise.

<Are you saying that the Robus form would break the Trol's hold over me?>

<Yes, I believe so.>

<Well, that's a really terrible design flaw on their part,> she replied with a mental chuckle. *<I mean, their entire point was to use Robus soldiers.>*

<I suspect the difference is your advanced telepathic abilities. Others likely wouldn't experience that same break,> Jasmine said. *<But I also don't think it's the difference of Robus versus normal Taran form. It might be the act of changing from one form to another.>*

Kira thought back to her encounter with Reya on Mysar. The alien had her cornered, but Kira regained control when she transformed into a Robus. Yet she retained that control when she shifted back to Taran.

<So, as long as I shift whenever I feel them taking control, I can keep them from overtaking me?>

<It's only a hypothesis,> Jasmine replied.

<Right now, that's all we have.>

— — —

Leon flipped through another batch of the test results that had yielded a false positive.

Jack and Tess had departed the lab for the evening, so he figured he might as well work in peace while Kira was meeting with her team.

The work felt fruitless, however. Nothing was showing up in the scans to explain why the automated review had flagged each of the records.

I really wish I knew what was going on so I could fix it.

He was about to dismiss the final record when something caught his eye. The person in question had been involved in the op three years prior when Nox entered Colonel Kaen—an event codenamed 'Starfall'.

Curious, Leon went back through the records of the people he'd already cleared.

"Well, shite." All of them had been involved in Operation Starfall.

But there was nothing biologically different about them. What might the trigger be? And why that *mission?*

He couldn't find any explanation in the mission logs— those publicly available to him, anyway.

All the same, it was the only lead he had. With no other recourse, he sent a message to Colonel Kaen with the find. If anyone could offer further insight, it would be him.

— — —

Kaen drummed his fingers on the desktop while he thought through the best way to approach the TSS about a joint op.

On the surface, using the *Conquest*'s TK weapon sounded like overkill. *He* knew it wasn't—not for nanoscopic beings whose tolerance for environmental conditions was unknown.

If we're going to destroy them, we need to vaporize the whole planet.

His thoughts were interrupted by a notification chirp, and a message from Leon popped up:

>>Sir, Operation Starfall three years ago, when Nox found you... all the people whose results are getting flagged by our automated checks were on that op. Can you think of any explanation?<<

Kaen froze in his chair. He hadn't wanted to think about that op, when so many had lost their lives. But knowing what he did now, he quickly realized exactly what must be causing the flags in Leon's test.

He initiated a video call with the scientist.

Leon was in his lab and picked up right away. "Sir, thank you for getting back to me so quickly."

Kaen nodded. "I should have seen the connection before." He looked down, taking a deep breath. He brought his gaze upward again. "The enemy used a biological weapon on us— an airborne toxin that attacked soft tissues. We lost a dozen soldiers before we were able to figure out what was going on. We needed to synthesize an antidote, and the most accessible lab with sufficient facilities was on a ship belonging to MTech."

"Surprise, surprise." Leon shook his head.

"The materials that were used as the base of the antidote were extracted from the plant life on Valta."

"It must have been based on some of MTech's earlier research into the planet's unique properties. And now that we know there are traces of valteron throughout the biosphere..."

Kaen nodded. "Did you and Kira trigger in the automated review?"

"No, we never went through that automated system," Leon replied. "Kira, obviously, is different; I didn't even bother to test her. Jack did a manual review of me earlier."

"Run yourself through the automation. If that triggers it, you'll have your answer."

Leon nodded pensively. "What about the soldiers who helped with the raid of the MTech lab?"

"They never ingested anything on the planet," Kaen replied. "We brought our own rations."

"That explains it." Leon nodded. "Thank you for the additional insights, sir. I'll look into this."

"Good work. Now, if you'll excuse me." Kaen ended the call. *At least we're one step closer to solving* one *of our mysteries.*

The next order of business wasn't a mystery, but rather a matter with a clear solution. After the ambiguity of the past two weeks, Kaen was happy to have a problem he could shoot to make it go away.

Now all he had to do was get the proper weapon.

With his thoughts as ordered as they'd ever be, Kaen called General Lucian—his best chance of getting what he needed. While an in-person plea would have been preferable, he was presently away from headquarters, and he couldn't delay submitting the request.

General Lucian answered the call after twenty seconds. "Colonel Kaen, I'm surprised to hear from you."

"It's been an eventful few days, sir."

He filled him in on the developments since they'd last spoken.

"That's quite a mess," he said when Kaen had finished.

"After talking through the options, my recommendation is

to destroy the dwarf planet in Gaelon," Kaen stated.

"I agree with that approach. These beings pose too great of a threat to be left unchecked."

Kaen nodded. "I don't think anything we have in the Guard arsenal is sufficient for the task, sir."

General Lucian leaned back in his chair and sighed. "What did you have in mind?"

"The TK weapon on the TSS *Conquest*."

"Did someone put you up to this?" the general demanded.

Kaen titled his head. "Sir?"

Lucian sighed. "I had a personal run-in with that ship about three years back."

"Oh, I didn't know," Kaen lied. He'd heard unconfirmed rumors that General Lucian had had a tense encounter with a senior TSS Agent during the conflict surrounding the Priesthood's transition from power. Word had it that he'd pissed off the wrong person, and the command of Orion Station was a way of putting him out to pasture before retirement. Based on the general's reaction, Kaen suspected there was some truth to the rumors.

"We've always made a point of keeping Guard operations separate from the TSS," Lucian stated.

"Part of the Guard's effectiveness is recognizing the proper tool for the job. In this case, I believe the thoroughness of the TK weapon is most appropriate."

"It's not the ship that gives me pause, but rather it's likely captain." Lucian shook his head. "I'll reach out to the TSS High Commander to see if they'll be able to assist."

CHAPTER 17

ELLEN HADN'T BEEN frightened many times in her life. As she thought about the alien beings lurking just outside the city, however, it took all of her willpower to keep from giving into the terror.

I'm supposed to be the rational advisor here. I can't give up. She took a few minutes alone in her office to settle her nerves. As she stared out of the window at the city below, she was reminded of the people she had sworn to protect.

She took one more slow, steady breath and released it. "I can do this," she whispered to herself.

As calm as she was going to get, Ellen stepped over to her desk to send a summons to Trisha and Fiona.

The two women arrived at Ellen's office a minute later, their faces drawn with concern.

"What's going on?" Fiona asked. "You've been acting strangely since that meeting with Edgar."

Ellen motioned for them to close the door, and they complied.

"We're in danger. The aliens are still on Mysar," she

explained as soon as her associates had taken a seat across from her.

"But Hale die—" Trisha began.

"I've spoken with trusted friends in the Guard and learned that the alien consciousness lives in pits, just like that one in the valley that Edgar told us about."

Fiona paled. "If that's nearby, then…"

"Reya had somewhere to escape to after leaving Hale," Ellen confirmed with a nod. "We need to assume that the aliens will take an offensive stance."

"Try to take people over again?" Fiona asked.

"Maybe. Or an attack," Ellen said, wishing she knew.

"Mysar has more of a military than Elusia, but we're not *that* well-armed," Trisha replied. "And certainly not prepared for a telepathic assault."

Ellen tossed her hands in the air. "Short of a planetary evacuation, which isn't close to realistic, the best advice I can offer is to have everyone stay in their homes. The fewer people we have congregated in one place, like all the workers in Dome 1, the less likely it will be for the aliens to hit everyone at once."

Trisha's eyes bugged out. "Stars! You don't think they'd really—"

"Everything I've heard suggests that these beings feed on pain and trauma. If they want to get stronger, they'll do whatever it takes to survive."

Fiona stood up. "Then we can't waste any time. I'll coordinate a peacekeeping plan with the military."

"I'll draft some media messaging," Trisha stated, rising more slowly. "Any other instructions?"

Ellen swallowed. *How did I get to be in charge? I was just supposed to be a political consultant!*

That was a matter to work through at another time. For the

present, if people were looking to her for leadership, it was her duty to offer it.

"I'll look over the media statement once you have it drafted. In the meantime, I'll see if I can get a status update on getting reinforcements to contain whatever's in that pit."

The two other women nodded their understanding and left to complete their tasks.

As soon as she was alone, Ellen called President Joris. It was well after working hours on Elusia, but if Ellen knew the president, he'd still be in his office.

Sure enough, he picked up almost right away.

"Hello, sir. Any word yet from the Guard about an action plan?"

"They're working on it. How are things there on Mysar?" Joris asked.

"I just filled in the two people I've been working with on the investigation. We're preparing for an attack, just in case."

"Too bad you didn't already find a suitable head of state replacement," he said with a slight smile.

Ellen sighed. "I'm a press secretary! And not even from this world! I shouldn't be making the kind of calls I've had to here."

"Someone has to do it," the president pointed out.

But does it have to be me? Ellen didn't have the energy to argue the point. "I'm doing what I can to prepare for the Guard."

"Good. An action plan is in the works now. We should know more soon."

"Yes, sir."

The president looked her in the eyes. "We're going to keep this system safe. Don't worry."

"I know."

— — —

A call from General Lucian illuminated on Kaen's desk.

"Sir," Kaen greeted.

"Colonel, I wish I had better news," Lucian replied. "The only available operators for the *Conquest*'s TK weapon are presently engaged in other pressing business. The soonest the TSS could have the ship in Gaelon is six days from now."

"We have less than four before we expect the Trols to act. That timeline is only speculation, but—"

"Delaying is a risk we can't take without knowing the Trol's intentions," Lucian interrupted. "You'll need to find another way to destroy that planet."

Kaen was about to protest, but he knew there wasn't anything else he could say. "We'll get the job done, sir."

"I have every confidence in you and your team. Good hunting." He ended the call.

Kaen slouched in his chair. *How else can we destroy the planet?*

— — —

Half an hour after the informal meeting with her team, Kira received another summons to meet with Sandren and Kaen, this time in the colonel's office.

<I hope this is the order to finally go blow things up. I'm going stir-crazy with this pent-up anticipation!> Kira said to Jasmine while she walked to the meeting.

<Yes, I've noticed that. If we don't head out right after this meeting, I'm going to suggest you go run laps.>

<A workout isn't going to relieve this anxiety.> She arrived at Kaen's office and found the door open.

Major Sandren was just settling into one of the visitor chairs, and Kaen was behind his desk. The colonel motioned Kira inside.

"Sirs," she greeted as she sat down.

"We're going to level with you, Captain," Kaen began. "We'd normally reserve the details for senior leadership, but you're deep enough into this matter that formalities have far less bearing."

Kira nodded. "Understood, sir."

"The TSS is unavailable to help us in time," the colonel stated. "That means we need to find another way to destroy the planet in Gaelon."

Kira's heart sank. "Do you have any ideas, sir?"

"We were hoping you might be able to offer insights into a potential weakness," Sandren replied.

"I…" Kira looked inward to Jasmine. *<When did my job description change from covert ops to planet-destroyer?>* she grumbled to the AI.

<We'll figure something out, don't worry.>

That was easy for the AI to say; she didn't have ties to the system in question. Kira had been trained to keep her personal feelings separate from the mission at hand, but that was easier said than done when her homeworld was on the line.

Valta was never just a singular planet. Mysar and Elusia were almost as much a part of her history as the house she'd grown up in—a small planetary system with cultural ties that persisted, no matter what was going on in the rest of the galaxy. They may not always have gotten along, but it was ultimately a matter of bickering siblings working out their growing pains. In the end, they would unite and be stronger for it.

But now, that future was on the line. The insidious force from Gaelon had upset the balance and was threatening to destroy everything the people in the Elvar Trinary had fought to create.

I won't let them. The thought was private, but Kira could tell Jasmine felt the same way. *We need a precise way to attack the aliens without harming anyone else.*

<*What about a variation of how you removed the entity from Colonel Kaen and Jared?*> the AI suggested.

<*That was dealing with an individual. We're talking about a planet here.*>

<*You don't need to go after the entire planet. All beings have a core.*>

<*You may be on to something there.*>

Kira realized she'd left the two officers hanging while she had the internal discussion with Jasmine. Only five seconds had passed in real-time, but that was a long time for her to be seemingly staring into space.

"My original advice was to blow up the planet with the biggest weapon we could get our hands on," Kira replied at last. "My opinion hasn't changed. However, there is another approach that might just be crazy enough to work."

"We're all ears," Kaen said.

"Well, we know that their key structures are composed of valteron," she said. "And we know which chemicals dissolve that mineral."

"You mean like when you removed the TR from me?" Kaen asked with a raised eyebrow.

"Exactly. If we could scale that up, we could launch a highly targeted attack."

"There's no way we could get sufficient quantities of those chemicals to dissolve a planet," Sandren stated.

Kira shook her head. "We wouldn't have to, sir. Just the pits and central chambers. That's the core of their power."

"Neurochemicals weren't designed to be administered to rocks. This isn't just injecting a syringe into someone," Kaen objected.

"We'd need a large-scale nebulizer and a ton of the chemicals. I know nothing about that, but I bet someone at MTech does."

The colonel's brow furrowed while he nodded with consideration. "Between Leon's former colleagues and Ellen's government contacts, I imagine we can connect with the right people."

"And, sir?" Kira paused until Kaen inclined his head. "I can stand up to the Trols, now that I have a better understanding of what we're facing. Jasmine and I have gone over everything that happened in Gaelon. I know what went wrong. Let me face them, and I'll make sure we get our weapon exactly where it will hit them hardest."

Kaen and Sandren exchanged glances.

"I don't see that we have another choice," Kaen said after a moment. "I'll make the preparations with MTech. Major, get to Mysar with Kira's team. We need to move quickly."

— — —

Leon shook his head. *Of course! Why didn't I think of that?*

Colonel Kaen's theory about the false positives had played out just like he had predicted. Anyone who'd been exposed to the MTech serum, or spent an appreciable amount of time on Valta, had been flagged in the system's automated review.

The good news was that they now knew the reason for the flags. The bad news was that he would still need to assess each account, since the very thing that resulted in a flag was precisely what they needed to be on the lookout for.

Fortunately, the testing was in the final stretch, so the work wouldn't be a burden for much longer.

With Tess and Jack out of the lab working on other things, Leon was just settling in for another session of manually reviewing records when Kaen appeared in the lab's doorway.

"Do you have a moment?" the colonel asked.

Leon doubted it was really a question. "Of course, sir."

"Did you get the results of your scan?" Kaen asked.

"Yes, it flagged me, just like you suspected."

"So, it's the trace amounts of valteron? I'm surprised no one was ever able to figure out what caused the Valtans' telepathic abilities before."

"We were always looking for the wrong thing," Leon said. "The mineral is in *everything* on the planet, so it never stood out."

"What makes the telepaths different?"

"The right neurochemistry, near as I can tell. In certain individuals, the valteron accumulates to form the neural bridge that enables telepathy. A random side effect."

"And such small traces that it never registered, without knowing where to look or what for." Kaen shook his head. "With everything we know, we still know so little."

Leon chuckled. "Humbling, isn't it?"

"Indeed, it is." The colonel paused. "That wasn't the reason for my visit, though I am glad to hear you solved the mystery. I needed to talk to you about the solution you developed for my condition with Nox."

"What about it, sir?"

"The neurochemical mixture—can it be scaled up?"

"You mean doses for a large number of people?" Leon clarified.

"No. More like make it into an industrial-strength aerosol."

The statement was so out of nowhere that it look Leon a moment to process the words. "I don't think that's possible. You could never control the dosing."

"This isn't for people," the colonel clarified. "We want to use it to dissolve the rock-like structures on Mysar and Gaelon. Since we can't get a super-weapon to blow up the whole planet, we need to take a more surgical approach."

"I wish I could help you, sir, but I would have no idea how to do that. Doctor Elric knows much more about the chemical mixture than I do."

"I'm not asking for you to perform the scaling, just to put me in touch with your former contacts."

Leon stared at him. "From MTech? You want to involve them in this?" he asked, not caring that his tone was far from deferential.

"I want to involve anyone who has the information and resources to accomplish this task in our timeframe, whether they work for MTech, the university, or anywhere else."

This is insane. Leon fought the impulse to say as much out loud. "It's *possible* that MTech would have the necessary chemicals to synthesize a large batch. If they do, it would be located in a supply cache outside the capital city on Mysar."

"Forward me the appropriate contacts, as best you can estimate. I'll coordinate with them and the Mysaran government to get some mining equipment."

Leon's eyes widened. "What for?"

Kaen cracked a smile. "To access their pit on Mysar. I doubt they'll let us in willingly, so we'll make our own door."

CHAPTER 18

THE INCOMING MESSAGE from Colonel Kaen caught Ellen by surprise.

Shite, what now? She set aside her review of the media summary Trisha had drafted.

"Colonel Kaen," she said, answering the call.

"The Guard is sending support to Mysar. It'll arrive in approximately sixteen hours."

Ellen did the math. It was the minimum travel time from headquarters to their location. "Thank you, Colonel."

"In preparation for their arrival, I have a request. Actually, several requests," Kaen went on.

"What can I do?"

"I hope you've made friends in the government, because you'll probably need to call in favors with everyone."

Ellen braced for it.

"Our plan is to make a chemical assault on the Trol pit in the valley," the colonel continued. "However, we'll need to source those chemicals on Mysar, and also create an alternate access point into the valley facility to directly deploy the solution."

"What do you have in mind?" Ellen asked.

"Drilling an access shaft," Kaen stated in a matter-of-fact tone.

"Drilling a...?" Ellen laughed. "Yeah, sure, if we had a *month*."

"You have sixteen hours, beginning now, to get the equipment to the site. We'll have twelve hours to drill, once we know the exact location."

Ellen almost choked on her breath. "That's an impossible timeline."

"I looked at your mining records, and the drills you have within range of the city can accomplish the project well within that time. Get the equipment in place and have operators standing by."

Taking a deep breath, Ellen composed herself. "This is critical to your plan?"

"It is."

"Then it will be ready," she stated with assurance she didn't feel.

"Good. And the second matter involves synthesizing a large batch of specific neurochemicals. We need to leverage any connections that government officials have with MTech. I have the names of contacts, but I don't know if they will take this threat seriously."

"I'll make sure the appropriate people get in touch."

"I'll leave you to it. Good luck." Kaen ended the call.

Shite, what did I just sign myself up for? Ellen shook her head.

She hit the comm on her desktop. "Trisha, Fiona, get Garett and the others. We have a new project."

— — —

Mysar glowed rusty orange against the black starscape out the *Raven*'s galley viewport. Kira and her team were dressed in their light armor, ready to head out.

Behind them, Sandren was consulting a tablet with the latest reports feeding in from Kaen and Ellen.

"Okay, everything should be in place for us," Sandren reported. "Mining equipment is en route to the valley where the pit is located, and a chemical cocktail is being brewed at the MTech lab."

"Sir, can we trust MTech to deliver?" Kira asked.

"Ellen has a government team overseeing it," the major replied. "The remaining MTech workers want this awful business behind them as much as anyone else. Honest people worked there, regardless of what the company was up to behind the scenes. Everyone is jumping at the chance to make things right."

Kira nodded. "Yes, sir."

"Kira, you and your team will head directly for Dome 5 to meet with Ellen's informant," Sandren continued. "We need to know the exact placement of the pit within the facility, and he's the only one we know of who's seen it."

"Speaking from experience," Kira began with a frown, "geography makes no sense when you're underground."

"This is true," Sandren replied, "but we have a map of the facility as part of the data Ellen and her people retrieved. The only problem is that the pit isn't noted on that map. If you can trace the route in the man's mind, we can apply that navigation to the map, which will then translate to the official geological survey."

"Understood, sir, I'll do my best," Kira acknowledged.

"What about the chemicals?" Nia questioned.

Sandren nodded pensively. "That's where things will get tricky—well, trick*ier*. The pit on Mysar and the one in Gaelon need to be hit simultaneously to make sure the Trols don't have time to relocate their consciousness to somewhere safe, assuming that's something they can do. The problem is that we need to load the chemicals onto space tankers to bring to Gaelon. The transit time will be cutting it dangerously close to the astral alignment time."

<We can't assume that alignment time means anything,> Kira commented to Jasmine. *<There's no way they'd construct something on this scale, and have it work only for a narrow window.>*

<I agree. Either our assumptions about the significance of the alignment are wrong, or...> the AI faded out.

<Or...?>

Jasmine's mental tone turned darker. *<Or they only need the alignment to* activate *the setup, and then alignment doesn't matter.>*

Kira's stomach twisted. *<That is the only explanation that would make sense.>*

"How do we deploy the chemicals in Gaelon?" Ari asked.

Kira returned her attention to the room. "I need to distract them."

Sandren nodded. "I don't know how to articulate that request, or if it's even reasonable, but we do need you to find a way to keep the interstellar transmitter from activating. We have no extra room in the timeline."

"I have an idea for how to do that, but I won't know for sure until I get down to Mysar," Kira replied.

"Then enough talking," Sandren stated. "I'll be coordinating activities from here on the *Raven*. As soon as the chemicals are loaded, we'll head to Gaelon. You need to gather the necessary information and get back here within two hours."

<No pressure,> Kira quipped to Jasmine.

<Only the fate of this system and maybe the entire Empire at stake. Nothing to worry about.>

Jesting aside, Kira was up for the challenge. She had full confidence that she would be able to extract the necessary map information from Ellen's informant, but learning the Trols' weakness would be much more difficult. When it came down to it, though, she had to succeed. Failure wasn't an option.

The team was dismissed from the galley, and they took the ladder down to the hangar so they could load into the shuttle in preparation for descent.

With Kyle and Nia at the front controls, Kira and Ari strapped into the back passenger area.

Nia examined the shuttle's navigation instructions. "Do you know anything about these dome districts, Kira?" she asked.

"We're going to Dome 5, right? I think it's the seedy part of town, from what I've heard. Not sure why an ex-government worker would be hanging out in those parts, but we'll go where we're told."

Once the *Raven* was in position, the shuttle dropped from the belly of the ship and descended through the atmosphere. Unlike on their previous visit, it was still broad daylight, and they were able to get a full view of the city's five domes as they approached. Kira tried to spot the valley from the air with no luck.

The shuttle set down a hundred meters from one of Dome 5's entrances, which was little more than an overhang and a sliding door.

Kira and her team stepped outside, and a wave of intense

heat washed over them.

"I really don't like this place," Nia muttered.

"You've been saying that about *everywhere* we've been recently," Kyle shot back.

She sighed. "Why can't we ever get assignments on planets with tropical beaches?"

Kira smiled. "Because we only go where there's trouble, and no one wants to cause a fuss in a paradise like that."

"Man, now I'm craving a drink with a tiny umbrella in it," Ari grumbled.

They stepped through the entry doorway into an intermediary space between the outside and the main set of interior doors.

Two sentries standing inside the door stiffened as the group approached the security checkpoint.

"State your business," the first sentry asked, placing a hand on his holstered sidearm as he surveyed the group's armor and weapons.

"Captain Kira Elsar with the Tararian Guard," she stated. "Our orders should have been filed this morning."

The sentry's colleague nodded.

"Yes, residents have been requested to stay in their homes. You should have a clear path to your destination," the first sentry replied.

"Thank you." Kira inclined her head and continued past them.

The dome's interior was less flashy than Kira would have imagined, for a civilization so reliant on technology to survive the planet's harsh environmental conditions. She'd seen pictures of the city before, but she realized those had probably been of the central districts. Any metropolis had an area that never made it onto the tourist brochures.

They followed a map depicted on their wristbands, since the light armor didn't include a faceplate with HUD. After a half-kilometer walk, they arrived at a five-story, plain concrete building.

"He… lives here?" Nia questioned with a raised eyebrow.

"You know as much as I do," Kira replied. "Come on."

The group headed inside. A reception desk was three meters from the door inside the small lobby, which was framed by hallways marked with stairway and elevator access.

Behind the front desk, the receptionist looked like she was about to call for backup. "Who are you?" she demanded.

"Tararian Guard. Ellen Calleti said she let you know we were coming."

"Yes, we got the request. You can't go up like that, though." The woman looked them over head to toe, her gaze lingering on their weapons.

"We don't go anywhere unarmed," Kira replied.

"Our policy—"

"It's not up for negotiation," Kira cut her off.

The receptionist folded her hands on the desktop. "Leave your weapons here, or I'll need to ask you to leave."

Kira glanced at her exasperated team members. <*We don't have time for this. Jasmine, I'm going to bend the rules. Hope that's okay.*>

<*Whatever accomplishes the mission,*> the AI replied. <*But you aren't going to hurt her, are you?*>

<*This is to* keep *me from hurting her.*>

Kira looked the receptionist in the eyes, locking her in a telepathic link. "*You're going to let us pass with our armor and weapons, just as they are,*" Kira said in her mind.

The woman blinked rapidly and placed a hand on the side of her head. "Uh, go on inside. Third floor."

Kira inclined her head. "Thank you.

"You just used telepathic control on her, didn't you?" Kyle whispered once they were beyond earshot of the front desk.

"Seemed preferable to a sonic blast," she replied.

Nia got a wistful look in her eyes. "Things would be so much easier if you could do that on all of our ops."

They boarded the elevator and took it to the third floor. As soon as they stepped out from the elevator car, a guard posted at the security gate sprang to his feet.

"Hey, you can't—!"

Before Kira could initiate a telepathic link, the three members of her team had rounded menacingly on the guard.

"Open the gate," Kira commanded, looking him in the eyes.

He fumbled for the controls, and the gate unlocked with a harsh buzz.

"Have a good afternoon," Kira said as she walked by.

When they were past him, she turned to her team. "We need to find this Edgar guy."

Nia consulted her wrist display. "This picture in his file is terrible, but we could probably identify him in the rec room, if he's there." She pointed to a directory on the wall with navigational arrows.

Kira nodded. "Let's check it out. If he's not there, he's probably in his room."

The rec room, as it turned out, was empty. During her brief glance inside, Kira also decided that it looked far from recreational.

<They did a number on him, for him to end up in a place like this,> she said to Jasmine.

<Hopefully you can make it right.>

<I will if I can.>

Having struck out in the first place they looked, the group continued on to the location of Edgar's assigned quarters, further into the facility from the elevator. To Kira's surprise, they didn't pass any nurses or orderlies.

"Shouldn't there be more people working here?" she commented to her team.

"Maybe they were sent home with the martial law state," Kyle speculated. "Just kept critical personnel."

"Clearly it was the B Team," Kira replied. "The security is a joke."

"In all fairness, they're not used to telepaths and Guard soldiers," Nia pointed out.

Ari nodded. "I'd be intimidated by me, just sayin'."

Kira rolled her eyes. When she checked the door numbers ahead of them, she saw they were close to Edgar's number. "Ah, there it is."

Bars covered the small window mounted in the door at Kira's eye level. Inside a narrow bunk was along the left wall and a man sat in a solitary chair facing a gated back window.

"Can you get the door open?" Kira asked Kyle.

He glanced at the electronic lock. "No problem."

Within ten seconds, the red light had turned blue.

"Wait here," Kira told her team.

She slowly opened the door to the room. "Hi, Edgar. May I come in?"

He made no indication that he'd heard her, so she stepped inside.

"My name is Kira. I want to talk with you about the pit beneath the facility in the valley."

Edgar went rigid in his chair. "The voices. The voices are evil!"

"I know." She crouched in front of the man and stared into his eyes. *"I'm here to help you,"* she told him in his mind.

He looked back at her, his eyes filled with longing. *"Make them go away,"* he thought in response.

"I'll try," Kira replied, not willing to promise an optimum outcome after what had happened with Cynthia Hale. *"But to do that, I need you to be open with me."*

Edgar nodded. *"Please. I'll do anything to make it stop."* The words in his mind were accompanied by a profound feeling of being trapped.

Kira thought back to Cynthia and how she had been defeated by that sense of confinement. Though it had been too late for Cynthia, Kira had a chance to save this man.

She set her jaw. *"Edgar, show me what you saw at the facility,"* she instructed telepathically.

"They don't want me to."

"Then we'll make them."

Kira dove into his mind. A tiny beacon flashed in her mind's eye, marking the information that Edgar wanted to share but was presently incapable of accessing. She clawed her way toward it, grasping the end of a thread. Holding onto the delicate strand that snaked through his mind, she traced the memory.

Flashes and bursts of emotion washed over her. Darkness. Fear. Whispers. Pain.

It filled her mind, burning behind her eyes.

Perspiration formed on Edgar's brow. *"They're too strong,"* he said in Kira's mind.

"No. We're stronger."

She redoubled her efforts, fighting deeper into his mind as the programming tried to yank the memory from her grasp. But Kira refused to let go. She forced back the mental blocks, skirting around them and pressing inward until the edges cracked.

As she got deeper, the sense of being trapped swelled within her.

They won't control me, and I won't let them have this man any longer.

With a final surge, Kira broke through the barriers guarding Edgar's hidden thoughts.

The desired memory hit her in a wave, threatening to overwhelm her in a torrent of negative thoughts.

"Stay with me, Edgar!" she shouted in the mind of the tortured man. Experiencing the storm that had been raging inside him, she was astonished he had been responsive at all.

Edgar cried out, piercing the silence in the small room.

Kira stayed focused on him as she sorted through the flood of memories. Somewhere, there was a clear path to show her what she needed to know.

At last, a series of images came to the surface. She recognized an exterior security door similar to the facility entrance she'd encountered on the Gaelon dwarf planet and then a control room—but this time, the doorway to the underground was already open.

A half-lit hallway stretched before her as she relived Edgar's memory. She walked in his footsteps, down the path, to a stairwell carved directly into the stone, as though the very rock had reformed in the desired shape.

The staircase descended on a wide spiral around a central column. There were no landings, so there was no sense of how deep it went, only that it was *far*.

After what seemed like an eternity in Edgar's mind, the end came into sight. An open door ahead led to a hallway hewn of the same stone as the stairwell. A persistent hum filled the air, which had made Edgar feel on edge, but he pressed forward.

Through the doorway was a lobby with four corridors

leading in different directions.

A middle-aged man with dark features stood in the middle of the lobby, sporting a pleased smirk. "This is a very important assignment," he said.

Kira watched through Edgar's eyes as he nodded. "I'm here to serve. What will I be doing, exactly?"

"Come with me." The other man led Edgar through a labyrinth of hallways.

Kira tracked the movements at first, but after seven turns, she found herself second-guessing her memory of the opening moves.

"Take notes," she said aloud to her team.

In Edgar's mind, she rewound the memory and began replaying it from the moment they left the lobby. "Second corridor from the left, third right..." She continued relaying the instructions until her host halted.

Kira held up her hand to indicate a pause to her team. Telepathically, she prodded Edgar to proceed.

Tears formed in his eyes. *"They want to hurt you,"* he told her.

"I won't let them."

"You aren't prepared for what's coming."

The memory advanced, but there were no more twisting hallways. Ahead, the path led to a cavern eerily similar to the one Kira had been to on Gaelon. At the center of a chamber, a black pit plummeted toward the core of the planet.

"This is it!" Kira told her team. "The pit is seven meters straight ahead of the doorway."

"Got it," Nia acknowledged.

Kira was about to disengage from the memory, having retrieved the information they needed, but whispers rose from the darkness. They beckoned to Edgar, and he cast his gaze around the room as he approached.

Once at the edge, Edgar looked downward to find the source of the whispers, but he couldn't see anything more than half a dozen meters into the hole.

"What is this?" he asked his guide.

"This is their home. We offer them an escape."

The whispers intensified. Fear welled inside Edgar, but he was frozen in place. Within the pit, jewels of light illuminated along the walls in strange patterns that he had never seen.

But Kira had. It was the same form as she'd seen replicated on Gaelon.

She wanted a better look, but Edgar tore his gaze from it, trying to back away from the pit. Something was holding him in place, and his limbs went rigid. Kira's own breath was forced from her chest as she relived the memory with him.

As the voices continued to swirl in her mind, one rose above the rest.

This one wasn't a memory.

"Kira, you've come back."

Kira's blood ran icy through her veins. She'd know that presence anywhere.

"Reya."

CHAPTER 19

KIRA COMPOSED HERSELF. She couldn't allow Reya to sense any fear or doubt. *"You're supposed to be dead."*

"Your weak mortal bodies can't contain us. Hale's death was a setback, not an end."

Kira had already figured as much, given what they'd discovered over the past several days. *"Where are you hiding?"* she asked.

"Whatever you're trying to do, it won't work," the alien replied.

"That wasn't an answer."

"You already know where I am. We know you're coming."

Kira was careful to guard her thoughts. She wasn't sure how she was communicating with the being, exactly, but she couldn't risk playing into the alien's figurative hands. The likely explanation was that Edgar was functioning as some sort of conduit.

"You should know by now that we won't stop until you're no longer a threat. Submit, and you don't have to die," Kira continued.

"*We will never submit to beings lesser than ourselves.*"

At least Kira could say she tried. Killing was never her first choice of action, but when an enemy wouldn't hear reason, it was the only path to take. Reya's stance made the decision to use deadly force a little easier.

"*In that case,*" Kira continued, "*we have nothing more to discuss.*"

"*We haven't given up on you, Kira. You can be so much more with us,*" Reya beckoned her with a musical lilt to its tone.

Kira mentally scoffed at the alien. "*You're still using that same line? I'm doing just fine on my own, thanks.*" She tried to sever the connection, but something was stopping her.

"*It wasn't a request,*" Reya bellowed, swelling in her mind. "*You will join us and fulfill your purpose.*"

"*No!*" Kira struggled against the mental vise closing in around her.

"*Obey! Kill your friends and come to us. You will become what you were meant to be.*"

Against her will, Kira's hand twitched toward her handgun, her gaze shifting to her team.

"*Yes, it will be so easy,*" Reya prodded. "*Slaughter them and relish their deaths.*"

"*Never!*" Kira tried to fight the being's immense telepathic influence, but she was already slipping deeper inside herself. Reya was trying to force her into a cage within her own mind, cut off from her outside senses. If Reya succeeded, Kira knew she would become another puppet for the being to control for its own ends.

<*Kira, where are you?*> a voice called out to her through the darkness.

<*Jasmine!*> Kira shouted back. <*Shift! We have to shift now.*>

<You've always initiated it, not me.>

<You know what state I was in the last time it almost happened. Do that. Hurry!> Kira pleaded as her strength faded. A moment later, she couldn't sense the AI.

She was alone in the darkness.

A burst of energy surged through her. She shredded the mental bonds that had shackled her and lashed out against Reya.

"You will not control me!" Kira snarled in her mind.

Reya recoiled from the sudden outburst, then gathered itself for another assault. *"Obey!"*

"It's too late, Reya. You've lost." Kira sent a telepathic spear toward her would-be captor, and Reya screamed in Kira's mind as the attack found its mark. *"We're coming for you, and you can't stop us."*

Before the alien could react, Kira sealed off the connection inside Edgar's mind. The aliens wouldn't be able to get to him again.

In front of her, Edgar was staring at Kira with a mixture of shock, confusion, and awe. His full attention was on her, but he looked like he wanted to get as far away as possible.

Kira looked down at her hand and noticed the claws poking through her gloves.

<Oh, right, that,> she said to Jasmine.

Then the pain hit.

"Argh!" Kira dropped halfway to the floor before she caught herself with her hands.

<A little help?> she asked the AI.

<I'm trying,> Jasmine assured her.

Ari was at Kira's side before the AI could say anything more. "Are you okay, Kira? Aside from the Robus thing, that is."

"Yeah," she told him, careful to avoid slicing him as he helped her to her feet. "Minus the part about all of my nerves feeling like they're on fire."

<Almost got it,> Jasmine stated. *<Ah! You should—>*

The claws receded, and Kira's skin tingled as the nanites reabsorbed.

"Well, that was unpleasant."

Edgar blinked slowly as he took her in, now appearing more fascinated than concerned that she'd just transformed into an alien creature before his eyes. Whatever meds they had him on must be good.

"What *are* you?" he finally asked.

"That's a long story." Kira crouched down to look into his eyes again. There was still fear in his gaze—not of her, but of the Trols' returning.

Kira inclined her head to Ari to let him know she was okay, and he returned to the hall. She brought her attention back to Edgar.

"They'll never leave me alone," Edgar told her through their telepathic link. *"They'll be back."*

"Not if we don't let them in," she replied in his mind.

She began weaving a permanent shield around his mind—so tight a mesh that the Trols would never be able to break through. As powerful as they thought they were, they didn't understand people's minds in all their complexities. Kira did, and with her knowledge, she would beat them.

But first, she could change the life of this one person who'd been robbed of his autonomy. They'd cast him aside when he was no longer needed as a temporary host, and it had left him a shell of his former self. Kira could fix him—she could do what she had wanted to do for Cynthia Hale but had been too late to accomplish. She could give him a second chance.

She finished weaving the mental shield and then carefully withdrew from Edgar's mind.

"They won't be able to hurt you now," she said as her telepathic parting words. Then aloud, "How do you feel?"

Edgar's eyes lit up. "They're gone! I can't hear them anymore!" he exclaimed.

"And you don't have to worry about them coming back," Kira promised with a smile. She stood up. "No more nightmares, Edgar."

He beamed at her. "I don't know how to thank you."

"None is needed. I'm just happy I could return your autonomy." She looked around the room. "I know this place isn't ideal, but I suggest you wait here until the threat has passed."

"You mean the threat from... them?" he asked.

Kira nodded. "We'll take care of them for good, though, don't worry." She turned to leave the room.

<I was correct about a shift breaking the Trols' hold on you,> Jasmine commented.

<Good thing, too, or we would have been toast.>

Kira's team was waiting in the hallway.

"The directions. We need to compare them to the facility map," she instructed them.

"Already on it," Kyle confirmed. He activated a holographic projection from his wrist, which depicted a three-dimensional model of the underground facility. "Based on your description, I believe it's here." He pointed to an out-of-the-way branch of the labyrinth with his free hand.

"That sounds right," Nia assessed. "The one on Gaelon was in a similar position relative to the entry and exit."

"It's the best guess and the only information we have without going inside," Kira said. "Send the information to

Sandren so he can coordinate with the drilling team."

"Aye." Kyle made entries on his wrist device. "Done."

Kira nodded. "Thanks. We should get out of here. I have other information I need to share."

Nia gave her a quizzical look. "That you learned from Edgar?"

Kira nodded. "I know what the Trols do."

"Like, all their secrets?" Kyle asked.

"No. How they operate. How they were able to make that planet," Kira clarified. "At least, I think I do."

"Care to enlighten us?" Nia prompted.

She shook her head. "Not here. We need to get back to the *Raven*."

"Who are you and what are you doing here?" a man said from down the hallway.

Kira spun around. She immediately recognized the middle-aged man with dark features as the guide from Edgar's memory. She drew her multi-handgun on the stun setting.

"Who are *you*?" she demanded.

The man raised his hands. "Garett Steckler. I work for the Mysaran government."

Ari pivoted to have his back to the man. "Is the gun really necessary?" he whispered in Kira's ear.

Kira looked the soldier in his eyes. "*I saw him in Edgar's memories. He was working with the Trols.*"

Understanding passed across Ari's face, and he pivoted back to face Garett while drawing his sidearm.

"What are you doing here, Garett?" Kira asked.

"Just checking in on a friend," he replied.

<*Or he learned that we were coming here and was trying to cover up information before we arrived,*> Jasmine said privately to Kira.

<If he's working with Ellen, he was cleared.>

<Leon said that the Mysarans weren't properly vetting the anomalous records because there were so many. He may still be subverted.>

<If he was on Ellen's team, then he knows everything we have planned!>

Kira's pulse spiked.

"I'm gonna need more than that," she said aloud to Garett.

She caught Nia's gaze across the hallway, since she was standing closest to the man. *"He may be subverted,"* Kira relayed to her telepathically. *"Subdue him."*

Nia spun around and had Garett in a tight hold with his hand pinned behind his back before he even knew what hit him. "Kira has some more questions for you," the soldier said.

Garett strained against her, but he was powerless in her grasp.

"Whoever you think I am or whatever you think I've done—"

"Save it," Kira said, stepping toward him. "I have other ways of getting the information I need."

She stared into Garett's eyes from an arm's length away. *"Tell me who you work for,"* she demanded in his mind and aloud.

He took a sharp breath and tried to turn his head away, but Nia kept him looking straight ahead.

"Tell me!" Kira shouted in his mind.

He didn't give in. Few could resist even her weakest commands, which meant he wasn't alone in his mind.

"Are you here, too, Reya?" Kira asked.

"You think there are only two of us?" a new voice replied. *"Oh, Kira, you have so much to learn."*

"Yeah, nope," Kira said aloud. "I don't have time for this shite right now." She ripped Garett from Nia's arms and shoved him down the hall. When she had a clean shot, she hit him with a sonic blast from her multi-handgun.

"Well, that's one way to take care of that," Ari said with a slight smile.

"We're on a tight timeline." Kira poked her head back into Edgar's room. "Change of plan, Edgar. We'll have someone take you to the government building in Dome 1 where no one will bother you. Grab your things."

"I… don't have anything," he replied.

"That makes it easy, then. Come on." She motioned him into the hall.

She nodded toward the unconscious man four meters away, and Ari grabbed Garett by the arms and dragged him into Edgar's room.

"We'll get the appropriate authorities to come retrieve him," Kira said as she closed and locked the door. "I hope it's not too late for him."

Nia gave a grim nod. "I'll be so happy when we don't have to deal with these Trols anymore."

Kira thought back to her conversation with Reya. "The Trols knew we were coming here to see Edgar. Could Garett have sabotaged the mining operation in some way?"

"We won't be able to question him until he wakes up," Nia said.

"Not necessarily." Kira crouched over Garett and gently slapped his cheek. "Garett! What did you do?"

He groaned and shifted on the ground. Kira forced one eye open with her thumb and index finger.

"*What did you do to the drill?*" she repeated telepathically.

A subconscious thought flitted by in his mind: *The regulator. Don't tell her about the regulator.*

Kira jumped to her feet. "Shite! How do we get in touch

with Ellen?"

— — —

"Okay, bring it in," Ellen instructed the team.

A portion of open office space had been transformed into a control center with workstations and a complement of frenzied staff. They'd been working for the past seventeen hours straight, first to get the equipment to the site, and now to maneuver it into position.

The final orders had just come through with the exact placement of the drilling location, which should land directly over the top of the underground cavern. Once the shaft was mined, they'd have an open pathway to pour down the chemical cocktail that should dissolve the valteron deposits hosting the alien beings.

"Drill is almost in position," Trisha reported. "Not that I know anything about drills. But that's what they tell me!"

"We've all been transformed into construction foremen today," Ellen replied with a slight smile.

"And lab technicians!" Fiona chimed in.

Ellen chuckled. "Yes, I suppose that's true."

"Speaking of which, where did Garett go?" Fiona questioned. "He was all excited about this drill earlier."

"Overseeing the chemical transfer," Trisha replied.

Fiona nodded. "If it's not one task, it's another."

Ellen settled into her chair, pleased to be working with such a capable team.

She watched the monitors displaying feeds from the remote sites as the workers moved the massive drilling laser into place. It, in theory, could cut through the entire planetary crust in a matter of hours. However, due to heat issues, and concerns about geological stability, they needed to go much slower.

If Ellen had her way, they'd just turn the drill on full blast to melt the alien nest, and be done with it. Apparently, though, the Guard wanted to stick with a more finessed version of exterminating the particular foe, and that involved the chemical mixture. All the same, laser incineration sounded much more satisfying.

On the monitor, the three-story drill finished maneuvering onto its hover platform. Giant spikes plunged into the ground to secure it in place, and the laser drill head pivoted downward.

"Ground team has given the all clear to go," Trisha announced.

Ellen took a deep breath. "All right. Let's—"

An incoming communication marked as 'urgent' and bearing Guard credentials lit up her monitor. "I should get this," she said, coming to attention. "Proceed with the drilling."

She rose from the workstation she'd co-opted in the central office and stepped into one of the conference call rooms along the adjacent hallway. Once situated, she answered the call.

Kira's face appeared. "Have you started drilling?" she asked frantically.

"Just gave the order. Wh—"

"Stop them!" she exclaimed.

"Why—"

"Now!"

Ellen ran from the conference room back to the central office. "Stop!" she shouted over the din. "The drill, shut it down!"

Trisha repeated the order to the drill team, and the monitor showed the glow fading from the laser head. "Care to explain?" she asked Ellen.

Ellen's face flushed. "Order came down from the Guard. Must be for a good reason. I'll get the details." She jogged back to where she'd accepted the call.

Kira was pacing back and forth on the screen.

"It's off," Ellen announced. "Now, what gives?"

Kira breathed a sigh of visible relief. "Garett. He was subverted. He did something with the regulator on the drill—I don't know what."

Ellen's head swam. "He...?" She leaned against the back wall of the tiny room. "The drill could have overheated and exploded."

"Can a regulator be fixed?" Kira asked.

"I'll have to ask the mechanics, but I imagine so."

"You have to get that drill going. Our timeline—"

"I know, Kira," Ellen interrupted. "We'll fix it in time." *Somehow...*

The Guard officer nodded. "There's one other thing. As soon as you get the drill sorted out, I need you to run some tests."

— — —

Coordinating so many moving pieces had Kaen in his element.

Reports were rolling in from the fleet sent to retrieve the chemical cocktail from Mysar about their progress filling the transport tanks, while the few armored ships the Guard could spare at the moment had been deployed as their escort. Everything was coming together, but the timing would be tight with the alignment.

A new message illuminated on Kaen's desktop. It was from the *Raven*, marked with Kira's access code.

"Captain," he greeted.

"Sir, we're on our way to Gaelon."

"I see the tankers are almost filled. MTech came through for us."

Kira nodded. "Yes, sir. There was a near-miss with sabotage involving the drill, but Ellen assured me the hole would be completed in time."

Now, that *I hadn't heard about.* "Are you sure everything is okay?" he asked.

"It has to be so it will be. Right, sir?"

Kaen smiled. "The Mysarans have proven themselves resourceful. I'll check in with them while you're in transit to make sure our timeline doesn't need to shift."

"Thank you, sir. I accounted for the estimated repair time when we established the planned release time tomorrow."

"Good." Kaen looked her over. "Did you have something else you wanted to discuss?"

"Sir, I think I know how the Trols have been able to build all of these things."

Kaen raised an eyebrow at the cryptic statement. "Explain."

"I mean," Kira continued, "we were wondering about their specialization as a species. They seem to have knowledge of nanotech, but not in the way we'd expect for beings that exist in that form. I think I figured it out, when I was interfacing with Edgar down on Mysar." She paused. "I believe they manipulate matter."

"Pardon?"

"Like, they don't actually *have* nanotech. They just manipulate what's there."

Kaen let the words sink in. "What about the telepathic receptors and the rock formations?"

She nodded. "I was thinking about that, too. Those are just

made out of valteron, a raw material. But when arranged in a particular pattern, it takes on a specific harmonic frequency that facilitates the properties we've observed."

"And the bioamplifier?"

"Tweaks to a simple biological form to accomplish the desired ends. I suspect their abilities to manipulate biological and inanimate materials must be limited, though, or else they wouldn't need genetic engineering to make 'vessels' out of Taran people."

Kaen folded his hands on his desktop. "It fits, Captain, but what evidence do you have? It's a bold claim about the capabilities of a race that already seems to be able to do things they shouldn't."

"Edgar's memories. The details he picked up," Kira explained. "It's different watching events through someone else's eyes. When I went to Gaelon, I was taking everything in as a Guard soldier. I've been to dozens of worlds and interacted with a number of races over the years. I'm used to accepting the unusual as normal. But Edgar—he spent his life on Mysar. For all the interaction he'd had with other species, he might put the cute, little cocoberas on Valta on the same foreign scariness level as a three-meter-tall tentacle monster. So when Edgar saw inside that facility, he picked up on things that I had glossed over because of my past experiences."

"Such as?" Kaen prompted.

"Well, my first clue was the stairs. When we were on Gaelon, I'd thought it was all poured concrete. Through Edgar's eyes, however, it was definitely stone—but there were no signs of the rock having been formed. It was just simply arranged in the final design."

"The facilities could have been different."

"That occurred to me, sir, so I looked up the footage from

our mission record. The exact type of rock is different, but it's not the concrete I'd originally thought it was. I verified that with the density readings. It's one of those little details that I didn't even think to look at."

"None of us did, apparently." Kaen's eyebrows drew together. "Were there other observations you gleaned from Edgar?"

Kira nodded. "Yes, sir. Two things. The first was a frequency—a hum—in the air. We never paid much attention to it on Gaelon because we're so used to background mechanical noise from ships and stations. The second thing was related to the walls around the pit. We didn't see anything on Gaelon, but when Edgar approached the pit, these weird lights appeared in the rock. There was a pattern in the forms—the same pattern we saw in the computer system architecture, and in how the landscape was arranged on Gaelon."

"We already knew that pattern had significance to them."

"But we didn't know why, sir. Seeing the minerals arranged in the pattern, I had Ellen get some MTech scientists to replicate the form with the valteron samples. Except the structures fell apart each time. That's when they made the connection that the waveform of the frequency was strikingly similar to the patterns formed by the minerals. So, they played the frequency while building the structures, and it all suddenly worked. The valteron structure held together."

Kaen leaned forward. "Are you sure?"

"It was small scale, but the lab results were verified," Kira confirmed.

"So, that frequency may have something to do with how the Gaelon planet operates," Kaen mused. "If we interrupt that sound…"

"It may break apart," Kira completed for him. "If the

chemicals alone don't do the trick, we can disrupt the bonds holding the rest of it together by playing an opposing soundwave."

"In theory."

"Yes, sir. It's only a theory. And there's a major complication: soundwaves don't travel in space, and we also don't have a big enough speaker, even if it did."

That's it! Kaen perked up. "We don't need actual sound."

"Sir?"

"Other types of signals—specifically, telepathic signals—don't require a physical medium for transfer. And that entire planet is designed to be one giant communication hub."

Kira raised an eyebrow. "Are you suggesting that I... *think* that frequency? We need to break up a physical object with a soundwave. Telepathy isn't the same thing."

"Doesn't valteron resonate with telepathic signals? To do that, it must convert the telepathic energy into actual physical vibrations."

"I guess, but..." Kira trailed off.

"You brought it up, Captain. Did you have something else in mind?"

Her expression changed to one of determination. "No, sir. I can do this."

CHAPTER 20

SHITE, WHY DID I ever agree to do this? Kira groaned inwardly as the *Raven* made its final approach into the Gaelon System.

<Not to be the voice of dissent, but it is a longshot,> Jasmine said in her mind.

<Thanks, Jasmine. That's really helpful,> Kira grumbled.

<Just being realistic. But I do think you should try.>

<I was going to try, regardless of what you think, but I'm glad to hear you don't think I'm completely *out of my mind.>*

<Oh, I do,> the AI replied with a dead serious tone. *<It just happens to be a brand of crazy I endorse. Go big, right?>*

Kira smiled. *<Always go big.>*

The plan was absurd any way Kira looked at it, but the nature of the enemy demanded an unconventional approach. She took a deep breath and went to meet her team in the galley.

"Ready?" Sandren asked when she entered.

Already seated at the table, the three members of her team were standing by to lend moral support.

Kira nodded to the major. "Let's do it."

"We're still a few minutes out from the strike time, but why don't you feel them out?" Sandren suggested. "You need to make sure you can get a solid connection."

"I'll give it a shot."

For lack of having someone's eyes to gaze into, Kira focused on the Gaelon dwarf planet visible through the viewport. *"Hello?"* she asked into the void.

She could sense the planet and the strange, constant hum, but no sentient presence met her probe.

"I know you're out there. I want to talk."

Silence.

"No response," she reported with a sigh.

"Hmm." Sandren stroked his chin. "Hopefully, once they realize we—" He cut off when a jolt rocked the *Raven*.

"Uh, what was that?" Ari asked no one in particular.

Kira looked around outside, but none of the other ships were visible with her naked eye. She reached out to magnify the view, but another jolt rocked them, powerful enough to make her stumble against the wall.

"That's not good."

Sandren ran toward the ladder. "I need to get to the bridge."

Kira followed him. "Is it something I did, I wonder?" she speculated while they climbed.

"I have no idea," the major replied. "Obviously, they know we're here now."

Once at the top of the ladder, they ran toward the bridge and were knocked sideways in the middle of the corridor.

"That was stronger than the last," Kira observed.

"I don't like that trend one bit."

Sandren was the first through the door. "What in the stars is going on?" he asked the captain and first officer.

"The ship is acting like we're caught in some sort of gravity well," Rodrick replied while he fought with the controls. "If I didn't know better, I'd say we were at the event horizon of a black hole."

Aleya shook her head. "Nothing about this makes any sense. Other ships are reporting the same thing. We're all being pulled toward the planet."

"Oooooh shite," Kira whispered.

Sandren turned to look at her, standing behind him. "What?"

"Remember how we said the gravity on the planet was too strong for something of its mass? What if they have some kind of massive gravity generator and they just cranked it up to the max?"

The others' faces drained.

"That would explain it," Rodrick said, "but I don't like where it's going."

"Artificial-grav at that scale is *really* unstable." Aleya shook her head. "I doubt they'd be able to keep this up for long without running into problems."

"And what would happen then?" Sandren asked.

"Stars if I know, but it'd be bad," the first officer replied.

"Pull back," Sandren ordered.

"We've tried, but navigation is, uh… not behaving," Rodrick said.

"Shite," Kira whispered to herself. "Sir?" She jerked her head toward the hall and left the bridge.

Sandren followed. "What?"

"What if the Trols figured out a way to remotely hack our ship's computers using the algorithms from the external processor we left behind?"

The major got that look in his eyes that he did whenever he was in crunch time. "We need to act before they get complete control." He ran back into the bridge. "All right, get ready to send those torpedoes. And, Kira, you're up. Time to get their attention and keep it."

"Yes, sir," she acknowledged.

<A foking gravity generator? Really?> she added privately to Jasmine while she followed Sandren back to the galley area.

<Pulling us out of orbit is a great way to ruin our day.>

<Except all of those tankers would explode on the surface and kill them anyway.>

<But we'd have a gruesome death,> Jasmine pointed out.

Kira caught on. *<And that might give them the energy to counteract our chemical assault.>*

<Sounds like a desperate move on their part, if that is their aim.>

<I don't intend to find out, either way.>

Kira reached the bottom of the ladder and then ran to the galley.

"What's going on?" Kyle asked.

"Gravity generator, we think. And they may have hacked our nav system," Kira replied. "But we're going to take them down first."

She stared at the planet out the viewport, extending her mind. *"No more playing. Let's have a chat."*

Her telepathic probe met only emptiness at first, and then a chorus of voices whispered in her mind. *"You'll still be ours."*

Kira tapped the side of her head to let Sandren know she'd made contact.

Sandren, in turn, pointed to the ticking clock for their synchronized strike. Kira would have to keep the Trols talking for another seventy seconds.

"Where did you come from?" she asked as a stall tactic.

"Far from here, and soon all will be ours," the chorus replied.

Another jolt shook the ship, and Kira steadied herself with her hands on the viewport's sill. *"I appreciate your ambition. In fact, I was just talking with a friend about how you need to go big or not bother. So, congrats on that."*

The aliens retreated slightly, as though caught off-guard by the casual tone—just like Kira had intended.

"We'd really like to stop fighting with you," she continued when they didn't reply. *"Except you're making that rather difficult."*

"Submit!" the chorus said in her mind.

Kira felt the tug of their power, but she held firm. *"See, we want that the other way around."*

"We will never work with inferior beings."

Feedback squealed on the ship's comm system, breaking Kira's focus. She covered her ears. "What was—"

"Transmitter on the planet just activated!" Aleya announced over the comm when the squeal subsided. "Signal is fifteen times prior recorded magnitude."

Sandren swore under his breath. "We need to shut that thing down!"

Shite! Kira struggled to clear her mind and restore the telepathic link. *"What are you trying to do?"* she asked the aliens.

They didn't reply, but the connection was reestablished; she could sense their satisfaction.

Kira checked the countdown clock: five seconds. *Let's see how long that smugness lasts.*

Sandren activated a magnification overlay on the viewport. The enhanced image showed a torpedo launching from the ship nearest the *Raven*, forming a thin, bright streak across the black. The trail continued through the planet's atmosphere, and then there was a moment of stillness.

An explosive plume flashed for a second, and then a shockwave rippled through the surrounding landscape. The torpedo had hit its mark, and systems registered that the capsule carrying the chemical cocktail had disintegrated like it was supposed to.

"I bet that got their attention," Kira said without taking her eyes off the viewport.

"Sorry," she continued through the telepathic link, *"that was rude of us to bust down the whole front door rather than knocking politely."*

The aliens roared in her mind—blind, directionless rage.

Kira smirked. *"Oh, wait, you enslaved a bunch of our people and then said you'd do it all again. Yeah, we're not here to play nice."*

— — —

"All right, it's almost time," Ellen said after checking the clock that had been synced with the Guard's master time. "How are we coming with that hole?"

"Survey puts it at a meter shy of breaking through the cavern roof. The Trols have to know we're close," Fiona reported.

"But even if they know exactly what we're doing, they have nowhere to run." Ellen smiled to herself.

They'd gotten lucky with many aspects of the plan. The rock was too dense to complete a geological survey ahead of time to make sure they were, in fact, positioned above the cavern and the pit it contained. At the halfway point, though, the scanning tech had been able to pick up the layers underneath. The drill's aim had been off by five meters, but they were able to adjust the angle so the final tunnel would bore out above the center of the pit.

While the Trols may be expecting an assault through the main tunnel—both due to the commotion on the surface, and because they were privy to the original components of the plan that Garett had known—the sonic component was a new addition, thanks to Kira's observation in Edgar's memories. When Ellen had suggested that Kira talk with him, she'd never dreamed such critical information would be gleaned. It was the advantage they needed to settle the score once and for all.

With the chemical tanks already rigged up, all that remained was to punch through the final rock in the cavern ceiling and drop the distribution hoses down the shaft.

Ellen consulted their timetable. "Okay, go!"

She released a long breath and splayed her fingers on the desktop while the drill made its final cut.

"We're through!" Trisha announced after getting confirmation from the drill team over the headset. "Dropping hoses—"

The ground rocked underneath the drill, trembling the camera.

"What's happening?" Ellen demanded.

On camera, the teams scrambled to untether the drill and move it away from the shaft. The scaffolding holding the drill flexed, threatening to collapse and block the hole.

"Shite!" Trisha exclaimed. "Is it going to cave in?"

A shrill squeal sounded over the comms, and Trisha ripped out her earpiece. "Transmission on all frequencies," she reported.

Fiona's eyes widened. "Are we too late? Was that the transmitter?"

Ellen didn't care to wait to find out. "Now! Release it now!"

Trisha swiveled back to her station. "Communication

band is clearing. Sending order."

The monitors showed the equipment around the drill site springing to life. The nebulizer activated, sending the chemical mixture through the tubes as a fine mist that would permeate the cavern walls beneath the drill site. Additional tubes, ending in spray nozzles, deployed a shower of chemicals to coat the walls of the pit.

The shaking stopped as quickly as it had begun.

"Is it... working?" Fiona asked cautiously.

"I don't know, but that ground is too unstable," Ellen replied. "Clear the site."

Trisha glanced over her shoulder. "Time to blast them?"

Ellen nodded. "As soon as everyone evacuates, activate the speakers."

— — —

Kira stared down at the dwarf planet, bolstering her connection to the alien collective within. *"You had your chance to live,"* she told them, *"but now force will be met with force."*

"And you will be overpowered," the aliens sneered back.

The Guard soldiers sitting around her in the galley went rigid.

"Sir?" she said to Sandren, hoping the situation wasn't what it appeared.

He took a choking breath, but remained immobilized.

Fok! Kira's connection to the Trols faltered as she tried to assess the state of her friends. "Stay with me!" she shouted, but they made no indication they could hear her.

<Jasmine, what about the crew on the other ships?>

<Unresponsive,> the AI replied.

<Shite, I need to break the hold somehow.>

<It'll break when we hit them with the sonic blast. You'll need to operate the equipment yourself—it doesn't have wireless controls for me to access.>

Kira broke eye contact with the planet to spot the auditory equipment that was set up on the galley table. As soon as she looked away from the viewport, the connection weakened.

<This won't work.>

<Yes, it will. You're stronger than them. Embrace your abilities.>

Jasmine's words refocused Kira. She knew exactly what she had to do.

She had to get angry.

All the hurt and confusion that had been swirling inside her since her nanite exposure flooded to the surface. She let it fuel a seething rage within.

Her nerves ignited—eyes illuminating orange as the nanites formed nails, fangs, and scaled armor. She wished there was something to slash, but telepathic destruction was in order on this particular day.

"You want to get to know your creation? Well, here I am!" she snarled.

Kira opened her mind to share her physical sensory experience. Her consciousness became one with the planet, integrated with the hub and carried through its tendrils, woven throughout the rest of the world. Thoughts were no longer her own, sharing everything linked through the hub.

Pain and anger led her to her transformation—to her power—but it was the other side of the spectrum that would lead to victory.

She drew on her sense of fulfillment in the Guard, her love for Leon, the bond she shared with her team—flooding the telepathic connection with the positive thoughts of what always gave her strength, but would be poison to the Trols.

They tried to pull back, but Kira's telepathic hold was complete. Sharing her happiness was just the opening volley, a ploy to catch them off-guard.

It was time to go in for the kill.

Kira activated the recording of the opposing soundwaves for the frequency resonating throughout the planet below.

The Trols shrieked in Kira's mind as she pelted them with the sound. Their pain washed over her, but nothing would stop her assault. They had done too much to her. She could take their pain, and she'd make sure they wouldn't be able to hurt anyone else again.

Her friends in the galley gasped as they regained control of themselves, freed from the shackles of their would-be masters.

Kira gritted her teeth as the shrieks in her mind intensified. The Trols had nowhere to go, try as they might. They struggled desperately to force their way into her mind and use her as a host, but she held them at bay behind an invisible wall.

"There's no escape," she told them. *"You won't stop yourselves, and so I must."*

She cranked up the volume of the frequency recording. It vibrated through her, filling her body and mind until she could hear nothing else.

In front of her, the view of the planet changed. No longer was it a peaceful orb. It trembled and seemed to glow with an inner light. Cracks formed across the surface, and giant, dark clouds billowed into space.

"Holy shite! It's working!" Ari exclaimed behind her, having been released from the aliens' hold.

"Hit it now!" Sandren ordered into the comm linked to the fleet.

The tanker ships surrounding the planet released their

secondary payload, spraying the chemical cocktail as a high-velocity mist around the debris. It was too large an area to get complete coverage, but they focused on the former location of the main transmitter, where the bulk of the valteron was concentrated.

As the mist connected with the rock particulates, the chorus of screams within Kira's mind diminished. She continued pelting them with the sound until no voices remained.

The telepathic link severed.

Outside, the former dwarf planet was no more than a loose cloud of dust.

"I think they're gone," Kira murmured. She shifted back to her normal state and turned off the recording of the sound frequency.

<*Wow. That was... intense,*> Jasmine said in her mind.

<*You okay?*> Kira asked the AI.

<*Yes, I went into my private place. I couldn't hear them, but I sensed what it was doing to you.*>

<*I wish I didn't have to hear them.*>

Jasmine gave her a mental hug. <*You did great, Kira. You did what needed to be done.*>

The mental exchange was interrupted by Nia wrapping Kira in a tight physical embrace.

"That was incredible!" her friend cheered.

"The fleet is no longer under the gravity's pull," Sandren reported. "The generator was destroyed along with the rest of the world."

Ari grinned at Kira. "Standing here, it looked like you stared at a planet until it exploded."

Kyle laughed. "Ultimate staring contest! The planet lost."

Kira cracked a smile to share in her team's enthusiasm, but

she was far too drained for it to be heartfelt. "There was a little more going on behind the scenes, but I'm glad it was a good show."

"No one else could have done that," Sandren said and clapped her on the shoulder. "Well done, Kira."

She gave a deferential nod. "All in a day's work."

CHAPTER 21

SOME EXPERIENCES ALWAYS lingered in the mind, and Kira could tell that what she'd just been through would be one of those. As she prepared for her official debriefing with Kaen and Sandren, she found herself with an uncharacteristic feeling of irresolution, despite the mission being complete.

<Why don't I feel closure?> she asked Jasmine.

The AI gave a mental shrug. *<The notion of 'closure' is still new to me. I understand the concept, but not the nuance of completing a task versus gaining some intangible sense of inner fulfillment.>*

<I've always gotten a buzz after an op. I don't know why this one is different.>

<Are you still worried about the bioamplifier gas giant and the worlds in the Elvar Trinary?>

<No,> Kira replied. *<Without that artificial world as a transmitter, those are harmless.>*

<Then maybe it's because we didn't learn what the Trols are,> Jasmine suggested. *<We never found out where they came from, or what they can do.>*

<And now we may never know.> Kira shook her head. *<It's actually kinda sad, when you think about it that way.>*

She traversed the halls to the conference room near Kaen's office. The two officers were just stepping inside as she approached.

"Good work," Kaen told her as she walked into the room. "That was smart thinking, with the connection."

"Thank you, sir." Kira tried to suppress the dissatisfaction that was gnawing at her.

They took their seats.

"We took some risks on this mission," Kaen began, "and not everything went how we would have liked. However, we defeated the enemy. That's what's important in the end."

So we think. The thought wasn't as private as Kira thought.

<You don't think that was the last of the them?> Jasmine asked in her mind.

<I...> Kira wasn't sure what to say. *<I think that I had a hand in something significant. And what happened needed to happen, but I'd hope that the resolution could be different if we found ourselves in a similar situation again.>*

Jasmine smiled in her mind. *<That's why I like you, Kira. You don't take this lightly.>*

<We altered the fate of a whole species. Regardless if they were the enemy, I'd hope that would give anyone pause.>

<It wouldn't. Not for everyone.>

Kira looked across the table at the two officers. *<Do they look at it the way I do?>*

<Maybe more than most,> Jasmine replied. *<If you have something you need to say, this is your one chance to say it.>*

Kira took a deep breath. "Have you given any thought to who these Trols were, sir?"

It was strange to use the past tense, but it fit, given the circumstances.

"A little," Kaen replied. "Why? Did you have something specific in mind?"

"Well," Kira folded her hands on the tabletop. "We know they had access to advanced technology, but nothing we've seen from them can cross space—they were using the Mysarans for all transportation. They were on Valta at one point, but Nox made it sound like they didn't start out there."

"Is there a question in there?" Sandren prompted.

"Well, sir. It just makes me wonder if they were the only ones of their kind."

The two men exchanged glances.

"That's not a line of questioning we want to go down at present," Kaen stated.

"Yes, sir. It's just—" Kira bit her tongue. "Never mind."

Sandren took a deep breath through his nose and released it. "What is it, Captain?"

"I was pondering whether beings as different as them and us could ever coexist. Are our frames of reference too different to ever truly understand each other?"

"I'd think not," Sandren jumped in. "I mean, they were able to jump in and assume people's lives with relative accuracy."

"But is it genuine understanding or just mimicry?" Kira countered. "After all, they treated people as a vessel to be controlled. How well could they understand us and find that to be acceptable?"

"There are plenty of sentient beings with their own bodies—Tarans included—who perform acts that violate the autonomy of others," Kaen pointed out. "Just because they showed no remorse doesn't mean that they didn't know it was wrong."

Kira nodded. "I like to hope that there's another group of

Trols out there who thrive on positive emotional energy."

Sandren cracked a smile. "That is a nice thought."

Kaen steepled his fingers. "And maybe more likely than not. There are counterpoints in nature, after all—like an antidote for poison."

Kira smiled. "I choose to believe we scored one for the good guys."

"We did," Kaen agreed. "And we'll always keep fighting for the good."

— — —

Leon paced back and forth in his quarters. He knew that Kira was back, but she had yet to reach out to him.

Debriefing, maybe? How long is that supposed to take?

He sighed. Consciously, he knew he was being impatient. All the same, he wanted to know what had happened in the Gaelon System. If Kira wasn't yet available to provide answers, maybe others were.

The central logs indicated that Kira was presently in a meeting with Kaen and Sandren, but the rest of Kira's team was in their quarters.

While he'd never presume to be in their inner circle, he had, perhaps, progressed beyond a generic outsider enough for them to fill in him on recent events. He headed for the team's quarters.

Kyle answered Leon's knock on the door. "Hey. Why are you here?"

"Sorry. I haven't been able to talk with Kira since you got back. Is she okay?"

The soldier softened. "Yeah, she's fine. Come in." He stepped aside.

That's a promising start!

Leon went in, and Nia and Ari got off their bunks.

"It's sweet of you to be worried about her," Nia said.

"Yeah, well, you were going up against a pretty nasty enemy," Leon replied.

"She was a pro," Ari said. "The rest of us got pinned like useless fools, but she kicked some major telepathic ass."

"Made it look like nothing," Kyle added. "After that performance, I think it's safe to say that she'll be actively embracing the new abilities from those nanites of hers."

Leon's stomach twisted, to his surprise. On the surface, he was thrilled that Kira had come to terms with the changes she'd undergone, but part of him had still been holding on to the person she used to be.

No, neither of us are those people anymore. We're here together now, as we are.

He took a deep breath. "So, what happened in Gaelon?"

"Crazy shite," Nia replied. "We had our plan all ready to go, and then they immobilized all of us."

"I thought they could only get to people with a TR?" Leon asked.

"Yeah, we did, too," Kyle admitted. "We were wrong."

They filled him in on Kira's heroism, using superlatives that may or may not have been appropriate for an official report.

"I know she was powerful, but that…" Kyle faded out at the end of his recounting.

Ari looked at him. "Kira's not just our leader anymore. She's a weapon unto herself."

Leon frowned in spite of himself. *Definitely not the innocent telepath I knew as a teenager.*

But even knowing how much she'd changed, that didn't

make him love her any less. If anything, he was even prouder to know that she'd grown so much and there was still a place for him in her life.

"I guess we'll all have to get used to those new abilities," Leon said.

Kyle snorted. "Yeah, to say the least."

"What's this, now?" Kira said from the doorway.

"Kira." Leon took her in.

She smiled at him, love in her gaze. "Hey. I was just coming to find you and saw that you were over here."

"How did the debrief go?" Nia asked.

"Debrief-y," she replied. "I don't think we'll ever have the complete story. Too many unknowns about where the Trols came from."

"Just glad they're gone," Nia muttered.

Kira looked down at the floor, then plastered on a forced smile. "Not our problem to worry about now." Her gaze met Leon's.

"Well, thanks for filling me in," he said to the team. "Catch you later."

"See you at dinner," Kira said to her team.

She and Leon exited into the hall and walked several meters to the nearest recess.

Kira pulled him out of view. "I missed you."

"I missed you, too."

Their lips met, and she relaxed against him. "It's nice having someone to come home to."

"From now on, you always will."

— — —

Nothing about Ellen's mission to Mysar had gone how she

expected. However, with the Trols' deceptiveness behind them, people on the world could finally begin rebuilding.

She looked around the conference table at Trisha and Fiona. The women had earned her trust in her brief time on Mysar, and she was happy they would have that foundation to build upon to help forge a lasting friendship between their worlds.

"I guess we can finally get back to why I was here," Ellen said after a moment.

"Right, figuring out our new leadership," Fiona said, followed by a sigh. "Garett is out of the running now."

Trisha's brow knitted. "How is he?"

"It'll be a process to rediscover himself," Ellen replied. "The TR has been dissolved, not that the Trols are around anymore to tap into it."

"All the same, I feel better knowing there aren't ticking time-bombs in our brains." Trisha shuddered.

"Couldn't agree with you more," Ellen said.

"I guess the task falls to us, then." Fiona drummed her fingers on the tabletop. "No small feat, selecting those who will determine the future of an independent planet."

"The bigger question is, do we need to stay a separate world?" Trisha asked.

Fiona smiled. "If recent events prove anything, it's that we're stronger together than we are alone. If the Elusians and Valtans are amenable, I move that we unite the Elvar Trinary with the Taran Empire once and for all."

Ellen pushed aside the work that sounded like it was about to become moot. "Do others feel the same way?"

Trisha shrugged. "The fact that no one has stepped up with a desire to hold a leadership position indicates to me that Mysarans are ready for a change in structure."

"We'd have a lot of details to work out," Ellen cautioned.

"Of course," Fiona acknowledged, "but this is our chance to build things the right way from the ground up."

Somehow my projects keep getting bigger and bigger. Ellen folded her hands on the desktop. "All right. Let's get to work."

— — —

When Kira had sworn revenge against Ari for all his pranks, she had known it would be a long game.

The stage was set. With the help of Sven, and a friend responsible for ordering fresh produce, Kira had procured all the materials she'd need to turn Ari into his own viral sensation on the Net.

She'd arranged an assortment of fresh flowers on the table, with a vase filled with water sitting nearby. Based on his assertion of making arrangements in the past, it'd drive him crazy seeing the incomplete task.

To top it off, Sven had helped rig a helium tank with a remote trigger under the table. All that she needed was to get Ari in place.

"Hey, Ari," Kira called over the local comm. "Could you meet me in the cafeteria on Deck 7? I think they need some help getting ready for the party later."

"Sure," the soldier replied. "On my way."

Kira crept into a closet with slotted doors that gave her a clear view of the table with the flowers, from where she would be able to film Ari in action using a combat recorder she'd disconnected from a helmet.

Shortly after she was in place, Ari entered the room. He looked around for other occupants and then wandered toward the table with the flowers.

<He's never going to take the bait,> Jasmine said in her mind.

<He will. Just wait.> Kira's eyes sparkled with glee.

After five seconds of staring at the vase and flowers, Ari sighed. "Can't just leave them here to wilt," he mumbled while picking up a bundle of stems.

Kira covered her mouth to keep in a snicker as he continued to arrange the flowers in the vase.

<Helium is flowing,> Jasmine confirmed in Kira's mind.

<I really hope he says something quote-worthy.>

Kira watched him work for another five minutes. At last, Ari stepped back to admire his handiwork.

He smiled. "That looks delightful," he said in a voice two octaves too high. "What the fok?" He clapped his hands over his mouth.

Kira busted out in uncontrollable laughter. *<'That looks delightful'?!>* she repeated in her mind to Jasmine, unable to speak aloud through the laughs. *<I couldn't have scripted anything better.>*

<I've already edited the footage and set it to that cheery song we picked out, if you'd like me to upload it to the Net,> Jasmine replied.

<Oh, yes. The universe needs to see this!>

<Venting the helium now. You can enter.>

Kira emerged from her hiding place with a grin on her face. "Hi, Ari. Whatcha up to?"

The soldier stepped in front of the flower vase. "Just, uh, helping out for the party," he said, his voice returning to normal.

"Oh, this?" Kira gave him a quizzical look, sneaking a peek behind him. "I thought you were on banner duty."

"Banners? Since when do we make banners for anything?"

"I'm sure it will seem appropriate after you get your first million hits." She smiled sweetly at him and then sauntered out of the room.

"Shite! You didn't..."

She glanced back over her shoulder. "I warned you."

Leaving Ari to fume, Kira traced the halls to the real party location, which would be getting underway in the next half hour. Nia had roped her into setup duties, but that was a welcome change of pace after being shot at and mind-controlled for the last two weeks.

She greeted her friend, and they began the final preparations for the celebrations ahead.

At the designated time, their colleagues arrived and began partaking in the copious refreshments.

Kira smiled at Leon when he entered and worked her way over to him. "This is a good chance to meet the support staff that keep this place running," she said around a mouthful of cheese and crackers. "Best to stay in their good graces."

"I can only imagine."

She introduced him to some people, and then eventually found herself surrounded by her team. Ari had decided to show his face, but he shot her an icy glare every chance he got. Kira couldn't wait to send a link of his new video to the rest of her team.

With Leon by her side and her friends around her, Kira's heart was filled with the sense of fulfillment and belonging she'd always desired.

Eventually, Kira's cup ran dry and she went to get another round. When she turned back to the group, she realized that Leon had wandered off. She spotted him several meters away, leaning against a table and staring out the viewport.

She moseyed over. "Hey, everything okay?"

"Yeah, sorry." He stood up and faced her.

"I thought you'd be more enthusiastic about joining in the celebrations."

Leon smiled and reached out for her hand. He squeezed it. "I couldn't be happier to be here with you."

"Then why isn't all of you here?" She tilted her head and gave him the questioning look that she'd perfected over their years together as teenagers.

He sighed, yielding to her just as she knew he would. "There's something that's been nagging at the back of my mind that I didn't want to bring up at the meeting."

"What's that?"

"When we drew that line in space from Gaelon to Valta, we only traced it the one direction. What if there was something else further out in space, beyond the Empire's territory?"

Kira frowned. "Like a Trol homeworld?"

"Yeah."

Kira took a deep breath. "If that's the case, then we just royally pissed them off."

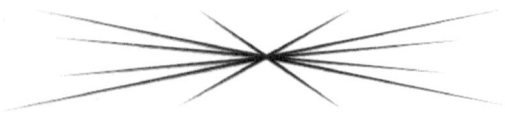

THE STORY CONTINUES IN *ENDGAME...*

Kira's nemeses are back, and they're after her home.

Captain Kira Elsar is adjusting to her new Robus abilities, but a series of strange attacks on the Tararian Guard's computer network throw her life into chaos.

A planet-sized ship appears out of nowhere, and it's heading straight for Kira's home system. With the lives of everyone in the Elvar Trinary—and Taran Empire—at stake, Kira embarks on a daring mission to stop the massive ship before it can attack.

Conventional weapons aren't enough to take down the alien vessel. Kira alone has the necessary abilities to defeat the Trols. This time it may be a one-way mission.

ALSO BY A.K. DUBOFF

Mindspace Series
Book 1: Infiltration
Book 2: Conspiracy
Book 3: Offensive
Book 4: Endgame

Cadicle Space Opera Series
Book 1: Rumors of War (Vol. 1-3)
Book 2: Web of Truth (Vol. 4)
Book 3: Crossroads of Fate (Vol. 5)
Book 4: Path of Justice (Vol. 6)
Book 5: Scions of Change (Vol. 7)

Dark Stars Trilogy
Book 1: Crystalline Space
Book 2: A Light in the Dark
Book 3: Masters of Fate

Troubled Space
Vol. 1: Brewing Trouble
Vol. 2: Stealing Trouble
Vol. 3: Making Trouble

AUTHOR'S NOTES

Thank you for reading this third book in the Mindspace series! I can't properly articulate how much it means to me to have your support.

I know this book was a little light on the combat action compared to the previous installments, but I hope you still enjoyed it! I wanted to explore a different kind of conflict that wasn't reliant solely in a brawn-based solution. Rest assured, the fourth book will be a suitably epic, action-y cap to this four-book arc :-D.

The original version of this book was my tenth novel, which made it a special milestone. I especially didn't think I'd have released ten novels in less than three years! That is the power in indie publishing.

It's been a fun experience reimaging this story in the Cadicle universe, and I'm thrilled by the fan reaction. While it's been a delicate balance to revisit the story without completely rewriting—since a story is never truly 'done'—but I'm happy that I had the opportunity to rework certain elements through this process. I'm also excited to see how parts of the story have changed as a result of the different technology employed in the overall story universe.

Anyone can be a writer, but this could never be my career without readers. I want to write books that *you* want to read. If you ever have any questions, ideas, or concerns, feel free to reach out to me directly. Let's explore new worlds together!

Special thanks to Craig, Jim, Leo, John, Kurt, Nick, Randy, Charlie, John, Curtis, and Ron for their draft review and insightful comments. Thank you to Jen McDonnell for editing and to all the LMPBN JIT readers. Many thanks also my proofing team for their incredible work behind the scenes.

I hope you're looking forward to continuing Kira's story in *Mindspace: Endgame*. Thank you again for reading!

ABOUT THE AUTHOR

A.K. (Amy) DuBoff has always loved science fiction in all its forms—books, movies, shows and games. If it involves outer space, even better!

Now a full-time author, Amy can frequently be found traveling the world. When she's not writing, she enjoys wine tasting, binge-watching TV series, and playing epic strategy board games.

To learn more or connect, visit www.amyduboff.com.